THE ART OF
BEAUTY

A Timeless Fairytale

Book One of the Spiritual Warrior Trilogy
The Adventures of Elandra

By

Ellen Ostroth

JMND
-PRESS-

First Edition: July 2019

THE ART OF
BEAUTY
A Timeless Fairytale

ACKNOWLEDGMENTS

My humble gratitude to a Higher Power, known to many and by many names. It's a real and wonderful thing to exist in the power of Unconditional Love. Why would we not?

Special love and thanks to my husband, Thane, for always being my hero, and to our beloved children Jesse, Nicole, Jennifer, and their children, spouses, and significant others for always being my inspiration. They knew I could do this, even when I did not. I love you all to the moon and back!

Many kudos to Roger Sakowsky for helping me get my creative "mojo" flowing again, and to Tasha Gavan for her vision. To Bessie Gantt, you are an amazing editor, friend, and wonderful validation for my inner self. The synchronicity has been amazing! Also, a super big thank you to Nicole Delgado of JMND Press for rescuing this techno-dinosaur.

To all my "Vibe Tribe," thanks for your patience and support. You know who you are, especially the amazing women who journeyed closely with me through this with valuable input and great humor. I love you.

Lastly, my heroine, Elandra, is named both for the Light (El) and my delight of a sister-in-law, Sandra. Honey, you were gone too soon and will always be loved.

PREFACE

Dear Reader,

Among these pages are fables and mysticisms. Many of my characters and the places in my books are based on actual mythological, theological, historical, philosophical and quantum theory teachings. The archetypical names and their essences are purposefully brought forward, as accurately as can be. Some of these energies are already very apparent in our world; others are simply very much needed.

Other than that, any similarity to any persons, places or events within my stories are coincidental. My books are Spiritual Fictions, intended to spark conversations, not cause harm.

That said let me introduce you to the Three Minds and the miracle that you are. The head, heart and gut make up a unified "magical" or "awoke" person. I call these the Three Minds of Human Wholeness. The goal of dysfunction is to keep these connections "offline". They must be open, and in alignment, for your Higher Self, Open Heart and Self-Empowerment to work optimally in your life. These books help examine these truths.

In Book I, The Art of Beauty, our three brave warrior women must use all their guts, courage and humor to fight their battles. This is known as the Gut or Stomach Mind, where we learn to believe and rely on the Godcraving within us.

In Book II, The Art of Betrayal, our skeptical heroine must use her intellect, instincts and uncommon senses to overcome old obstacles and clarify her perceptions, or lose everything. This is our Brain Mind, where we all house the forgotten power of our Godspark.

The Art of Being, Book III, has our traveling caravan of women relying strongly on faith to fuel hope which empowers their beliefs, which are worth fighting for. They must each reluctantly explore their Heart Minds or Godheart, the place of all true love.

These three Spiritual Minds are available in us all. I wish you much divine guidance in achieving moksha, which is your own spiritual unification. I promise you it will be there.

In Joy,
Ellen

"Since love grows within you,
Beauty grows within you, too,
Because love is the beauty of the soul."
St. Augustine

CAST OF CHARACTERS

Elandra	Warrior woman at personal war with God
Aurora/Rory	Half-lioness and the heiress to the throne of Mythoses
Skye	Good faery and friend to Elandra and Aurora
Queen Boudica	Temporary queen and steward. Elandra's earthly mentor
Marisha	A fellow traveler the trinity befriends along the way
Corban	Vizier to the queen. Boudica's loving consort and advisor
Aethelwyn	Skye's beloved horse

Seven Heavenly Goddess Virtues and Family

Prudence	The mother virtue—sagacity, diligence, humility, and discipline
Justice	Gratitude, nonjudgment, forgiveness, equanimity, right choices
Fortitude	Brave endurance, persistent ethics, courage
Temperance	Moderation of desires including sensual, purity of motive
Faith	Higher belief, compassion, contentment
Hope	Reverence, modesty—hope begets faith
Charity	Generosity, mercy, kindness
Veritas	Birth mother of the seven virtues and goddess of truth

| Patience & Perseverance | Twin daughters of Prudence, they assist Hope |

The Good Queen Mothers

Elbereth	Queen of benevolence, rules moon and stars
Clementia	Queen of kindness, Quan Yin lineage, grandmother to the others
Eithne	Queen of splendor, advisor to Heaven
Celestia	Queen of guardian angels, Elandra's celestial guide
Seelie Queen	Queen of elemental earth and the Fae of Light
Good Mother	Title of great respect for all female mystical sages

The Other Good People

Kumari	Princess Devi, queen of the Devas and prophesized queen of worldly love and peace
Chasca	Goddess of dawn and twilight, temple priestess
Mahaveritas	Prince, Kumari's tutor, Rory's twin flame, son of Veritas
Sister Phaena	Assistant to Elbereth, messenger of the Heavens
Shai	Genderless deity also known as Fate, enjoys playing the virtues and sins against each other
Bec	Guardian of sacred wells and goddess of wisdom
Aum	Universal mother, primordial energy

Balance & Harmony	Seductive nymphet water elementals, daughters of Bec
Valeria & Kyrie	Twin Angels of Death they take souls to final rest
Alala	Warrior goddess, she starts and ends battles with her war cry

Kingdom of Mythoses
Where It All Began

Artoria	Aurora's ancestor and a cruel princess
Kratos	Artoria's murderous consort and lunatic god
Elanhandra	Priestess and tutor of small children, spiritual healer
Elthaneos	Elanhandra's husband and eternal twin flame
Kaitlin & Quentin	Elanhandra's favorite young students
King Zeus	Father and ruler of gods, goddesses and their kingdom, Kratos's father
King Neptune	Sea god who destroys Mythoses and starts the prophecy
Venelia	Wife of Neptune and benefactor to Mythoses

The "Bad Guys"

Lucifer	Fallen archangel who controls the seven deadly sins
Unseelie King	Dark and treacherous king of the dark Fae people, the "unholy"
Evil Triplets	Unholy trinity of minor goddesses—

	they torture the dying
Nyx	Beautiful and powerful goddess of the night who brings fear

Seven Deadly Sins
Powerful Demons Used to Enslave Humans

Wrath	Competes mainly against the goddess Hope
Pride/Vanity	Competes mainly against the goddess Prudence
Sloth	Competes mainly against the goddess Fortitude
Envy	Competes mainly against the goddess Faith
Greed	Competes mainly against the goddess Charity
Lust	Competes mainly against the goddess Temperance
Gluttony	Competes mainly against the goddess Justice

PROLOGUE

Can a Wounded Warrior Be Restored?

Can a trio of warrior women outsmart and outrace the devil himself? They are sure about to try.

Wishing to restore her adopted homeland, Elandra engages the aid of her best friends, Skye and Aurora. Elandra is part angelic, and Skye is half-faery. Aurora is half-lioness and heiress to the kingdom. Each was abandoned as a child, causing deep wounds but also special powers. Each brings a warrior's skill to the mission. Each is set to mastering nearly insurmountable tasks. Should they fail in their quest, the mystical island kingdom of Mythoses is forever doomed.

The trio is presented with several hard decisions along the way. A wrong choice could ruin everything. Can the handsome prince be trusted? Should they befriend the small waif in search of her lost brother? What is the temple priestess truly after? Are they even certain they can trust each other?

Elandra struggles to keep her wits about her, even as she and the others wander through the seductive magicks of lust, love, and lessons. The darkest forces on Earth stay hot on their trail. The devil is salivating, confident of his conquests. He is certain these warriors' souls are his!

Heaven tries to help by sending down celestial reinforcements, but they are bound by universal laws that evil does not abide by.

Who will return home and who will be lost?

THE UNITED TRINITY

Elandra gazed at the beautiful woman and wondered why she did not feel more envious. Maybe it was because the woman was trying to skewer her with a wicked-looking sword.

With a sigh, Elandra balanced nearly weightless on the balls of her feet. She hefted her own viciously sharp sword and prepared to parry and thrust. Swordplay was not Elandra's favorite pastime, but she was exceptionally good at it.

"Attention, Elandra! If I had half a mind to, you'd be drawn, quartered, and I'd be back at the castle with a draft of lager, warming myself before the fire."

The woman, Queen Boudica, smiled grimly. The truth was Elandra was her most formidable student.

"Yes, Boudica," replied Elandra. She pushed thoughts of boredom from her mind and prepared to square off again against her relentless tutor, one final time.

Focused on the opponent in front of her, Elandra froze as a pointed blade was placed across her throat from behind. A sinewy arm snaked across her shoulder. She was pulled into a defenseless position. Dang!

The tittering, bird-like laughter behind her was immediately recognizable. Skye, her half-faery friend, leaned in and kissed Elandra's cheek.

"Got you, my fierce friend." Then Skye released her, and with a grin, Elandra slipped her own arm around the little sprite and hugged her in greeting.

"That's a good lesson to remember," Boudica said. "Your worst dangers will usually sneak up behind you, totally unexpected, even as you are focused on the challenges in front of you."

Boudica wasn't about to miss out on a good teaching moment. She pushed away the slight annoyance she felt at the intrusion into her self-defense lesson with Elandra. The queen knew Elandra had plenty of dangers ahead of her.

"Oh, come. Come! That's enough for now." Skye plucked at Elandra's sleeve, while turning her clear blue eyes to Queen Boudica, in a silent plea to dismiss the lesson.

Boudica sighed. These young women tugged at her heart, even as she tried to steel herself against caring for them. Loss was a part of life. Something these girls would experience soon enough.

"Oh, go! Get on with the two of you, then." Her smile belied her scowling tone.

Skye shot the formidable pre-Amazonian a quick salute. Elandra dropped momentarily into a deep curtsy, acknowledgment of her worthy opponent and mentor.

With unconcealed grins, the young woman scampered off, Elandra's sword back in its scabbard. Skye's wicked dagger seemed to have vanished into thin air.

Boudica's eyes narrowed in thought as she watched the two departing figures. Yes, time was nearing. Elandra would soon be departing on her quest and then only God could help her. The enormity of what lay ahead weighed heavily on the queen's heart. She realized that a small piece of that sorrow was her own desire to once again lead an epic quest of self-discovery. If Elandra and her friends were successful, this tiny kingdom, a little jewel where time had stood still for so long, would again thrive, the prophecy fulfilled. She sighed. She supposed that would have to be enough for her.

Queen Boudica turned her eyes upward and made note of the gathering thunderclouds. There were storms ahead, indeed!

****

Laughing, the two friends burst into the round turret room that was Elandra's cozy sanctuary.

"So, how was swordplay with Bodacious Boudica today?" Skye asked. The girls burst into giggles.

Boudica was a warrior-goddess of unmatched skills. She was also head priestess of the kingdom in which no true monarchy currently sat upon the throne. The title "queen" was used out of respect.

The queen was also a seer. She could know—see and hear—other's thoughts and intents. Now, even at a distance, she sensed Elandra and Sky's laughter, and she did not appreciate it.

The priestess had earned the nickname Bodacious Boudica not just for her legendary figure and strength, but because she could fully channel the sensuous energy of the great serpent, Lilith. The priestess was a seductress with a siren's song and a lover's touch. It was said her sexual prowess had done more to disarm warring adversaries than even her wicked sword skills.

"Another sort of *swordplay*," Skye said of it now in the turret room, sending Elandra a knowing wink that caused more fits of laughter.

"Hey! Hey, now!" The heavy wooden door flung open. The third in this trinity of friends stood framed in the doorway, hands on hips.

"All this laughter, and me missing the jokes." The fiery, red-headed woman strode into the room.

"Hi, Rory!" Elandra and Skye greeted her simultaneously, big grins on their faces. Rory was actually Princess Aurora, the last royal blood of their small but idyllic kingdom, now comprised of the only survivors through time from the kingdom's dark madness centuries earlier.

It was for the kingdom, and the fulfillment of the prophecy, that these three women were being trained in battle skills. The king's lineage had been meticulously tracked, and Aurora was the last of the true royals. In order for Aurora to rightfully ascend to her throne, she had to undertake a quest. She did not really know what, where or why, but felt nonplussed by these issues in her eagerness to be off on her first real adventure. The journey details were vague, the roads unknown and her chances of success mostly wishful thinking. But then, what epic journey ever started any other way?

Aurora would have to regain great powers before she would be deemed fit to rule. Elandra and Skye would be with her every step of the way to offer whatever assistance—or protection—they could provide. They were a formidable trio. Aurora was a true huntress. Elandra was a famed warrior and Skye an unsurpassed healer.

Unknown to Elandra and Skye, they too would have major roles to fulfill and lessons of their own to struggle with. This journey would be fraught with dangers for them all. And Elandra couldn't wait to get started! She knew Aurora would be remembered in history as a fair and compassionate queen—so unlike Atoria, the murderous family royal who had come before her such a long, long time before.

THE EARLY KINGDOM OF MYTHOSES

On a tired exhale, Queen Boudica began to study the ancient scrolls again. She was locked in her chambers and had asked to be left alone. Someone knowledgeable had survived the demolition of the Kingdom of Mythoses and then scribed it all. Boudica thought it had been Elandra's ancestor, scribed as her gospel, at a later time. Perhaps even in a future life. These were the only known written records. These scrolls were the last hope to restore the royal kingdom. She adjusted her candlelight and began to read.

Where it all began, eons ago…

Young and wistful, Artoria gazed moodily upon her island kingdom of Mythoses. Mythoses had been mysteriously drawn into the third dimension by the magical energy of the Fae, at the request of King Zeus. It had been intended as a prototype for a future kingdom called Camelot. Princess Atoria's destiny was to be its beloved queen one day and to keep these prosperous lands happy. An unseen, but fated flaw in Atoria was also prophesized to ruin everything.

Artoria had a dark, murderous heart.

The princess was quite deranged in fact, and in her madness, she did not wish to wait for her parents to retire the throne. Her impatience simmered. Her need for absolute control might accomplish great wealth of coin throughout her future reign, but her current life was bereft of love and human relationships. Her consort, Kratos, the lascivious demi-god of war and pageantry, only used her body. He was incubus to her succubus. As such, they fed on, as well as shared, their corrupted kundalini powers. Their coupling involved no lovemaking, only lust and control.

Their intoxicating connection resulted in an electromagnetic charge in the air and water of a sexual love, of sorts, and the island kingdom thrived. The people were content, although the gentlest among them—the farmers, fishers, bakers, and harvesters—declined to visit the castle. Indeed, they invoked protections against an evil eye whenever they came within sight of the royal court. The people were afraid bad magicks were at work within the castle walls.

****

Enthralled, Queen Boudica continued to read:

For all our wisdom we were fools. We forgot that darkness still existed within the world. The simple truth is human beings are so easily lulled by an easy life, and so we were willing to ignore the seething darkness.

I am scribing this with the benefit of perfect hindsight. I was known as Elanhandra, priestess, healer, and tutor. The future mad Queen Artoria was then only a princess. Let me tell you the story…

That ethereal time of the Kingdom of Mythoses had never been seen before, nor has it since. Even the famed Camelot soon fell in upon its own greed and treachery, like Mythoses, and was swept from our Earth. I have witnessed it all. This raging destruction of the Kingdom of Mythoses set a pattern of destruction. It seemed to suck all the light from the world. Glorious with its spires of shining light and shimmering air, the Kingdom of Mythoses belied its future ruler's madness. Laughter was the food of the people. Love had pumped their hearts. True knowledge had always enlightened their heads, and yet, all was lost.

You see, all beings are hatched into supple growing bodies. My greatest joy was rebirthing the wee ones into their true selves. From infancy to adulthood, the limbs and brains and hearts stretch and grow. The body is strong. Beautiful. It is the best shelter for the mind. We of the Kingdom of Mythoses had maintained our body vessels. We had swept our bodies clean with sacred light and coated them with trinkets. We'd shut the doors to our minds at night to keep them safe and secure. An amazing thing, the body. Although, often too cumbersome to wear.

I was generally out of body. I so enjoyed the sunshine on my nakedness, for God did not create the sun to harm us. This I have always known. The gods and goddesses can attest. Our beautiful isle Kingdom of Mythoses is now a land swallowed whole by water. Naturally, I had always loved the feel of the waves, too. And of course, the kiss!

What is a kiss without lips to press against another? Ah. My husband, Elthaneos! I can still feel my body, all the way back in time to where it lay, our lips touching. But my thoughts stray.

I was late for the rebirthing that day! I remember the scolding from my beloved garden.

"Elanhandra, hurry! You daydream and the hatchlings are incorrigible."

"Sorry, my dearest flower. I forget myself," I said and hurried along. *Talking flowers,* I was musing. *What would a world be without them?*

"Ah, my bright sprites! Are you quite set for a dunking today?" I greeted the seven small beings who were gathering eagerly around me at the edge of the basin. From knee-high to waist-high they glowed with the promise of a party. Around us gathered six more identical groups.

The egg-shaped dunking pool gradually sloped to four feet deep at its center. It was lit by Father Sun to capture the blue rays of healing. That day, seven priests and priestesses were assisting to submerge the wee buttons in order to heal all their past life traumas at one time. Fasting was required. The little ones had not eaten for three days. Instead, they had been schooled on the ways of their "becoming."

It was not always so. Once upon a time, the God soul sparks that splintered off from Source were immune to such tarnish. But out of the nothingness, darkness came. It fractured the holy light. It sent dark sparks, and like bad seeds, they grew.

So that day, in the healing blue rays of the water, those small tarnished souls were scrubbed clean. Squeaky clean. Original knowledge was then restored and the Kingdom of Mythoses was to continue its idyllic existence. We were people who created. We magnified. We multiplied—those useful bodies again! We had long ago eradicated any dark. So we had no fear. That was a time of grand faith. A time of great naiveté.

Hard to be both solemn and gleeful, but we were. We seven glided into the waters, and one by one the wee ones were drawn in, passed along and dunked not once, but seven times. Some sputtered. Some sneezed. All laughed, for this was indeed a happy time.

Wrapped in soft, thick towels after the dunking, the wee ones were now initiated. They could ask their questions.

"Why, my lady, do you glow and I do not?" said

Kaitlin.

"I am out of body. What you see is my luminous self. Pure energy and sacred light. In this form, I have no bounds in time or space. There is no limit to where I can go or what I can become."

"Does this mean I can fly now?" asked Quentin, furrowing his small brow under his unruly mass of red hair.

"Soon, dear heart. Soon," I said. "I am not bound by gravity. Many of us are not. But we are of the most Ancient Ones, from a time before it was possible for a soul to tarnish. You have a few things to learn and a millennium to learn them, but you shall fly. Meanwhile, there are whirlyraptors."

Forty-nine bright little faces lit up.

Whirlyraptors were an artless contraption, but fun. The children loved them. Made from a lightweight metal, they were bell-shaped with a swing seat. One sat upon the seat and the sides went upward, crisscrossing at the top, to form fast-moving blades. Once seated, one simply held onto the sides and intended to fly.

The whirlyraptors were entirely steered by intent. *But then, what is not?*

As the wee ones scampered to get ready for their long-awaited meal, I heard my name called.

"Elanhandra! Elan…Love..."

"Ah, Elthaneos, you handsome dream. How does the world live within you today?" I smiled at my beloved husband.

"Better, now that I am at one with you." Elthaneos, stepping closer, merged his light energy within mine.

"If I were in body I would blush, so cheeky you are,

and in plain sight of everyone." I giggled.

Elthaneos rocked with laughter. His gentle energy gyrated within me, and my mind went briefly to our satiated and interlocked bodies, resting contently upon our luscious bed. We had left our bodies under the warm glow of matted light fibers. Our room would still be awash in all the colors of the rainbow. Soft music would still be lilting. We elders rested our bodies while we worked—if dunking the wee ones could be considered work.

"I must hurry, dearest, for the forty-nine newest sprites are now officially a part of our isle family in the Kingdom of Mythoses," I said. "Our queen and king will be awaiting a feast in celebration."

"Elan—" Elthaneos said and then hesitated.

My radar shot into cautious concern. It was not often the Dunking Day brought anything but joy.

"What is it, dearest?" My concern was almost petulance, so ready was I for a warming fire and a goblet of rich, red wine.

"Our princess has been acting rather, bewitched, shall we say. She has been coveting, and therefore consuming, the sexual energies of the plants and animals. That has awakened a deep, rutting lust within her. I fear her consort can no longer satisfy her appetites."

I glanced around in caution. These were blasphemous words, but my heart knew them to be true. The royal chaos around the sudden arrival of the lunatic god Kratos had prevented anyone at the time from understanding that the mutilation and sacrifice of cows, goats, and sheep had been the depraved work of their own precious princess. She was filling her deviant appetites. It had not been a lone wolf or other predator. It had not been a wild predator at all. Certainly not one who had vanished from the kingdom as suddenly and ravenously as it had appeared, like others assumed. Kratos' appearance had temporarily tempered Artoria's bloodlust. Her desire at least temporarily curbed, contented life continued. Only Elthaneos, the lone descendant of both heavenly and Fae warriors, had been suspicious of who the true culprit was.

"Milady. Milady!" The flowers tittered and spun. "Hurry, for the horn has sounded. The feast has begun. You are late to join the other priests and priestesses along with your newly polished sprites at the queen and king's table."

With a start, I realized the time. The sun was sinking into the waters on my left. The sky was aglow in gold. Dinner would soon be served.

"Elthaneos, darling one, I must hurry and don my body and my garments and then hurry to the Great Hall. Jovial partiers that they are, our lieges will save me no wine."

My beloved grinned his handsomely boyish grin. With a slight slurping sound, our comingled energies pulled apart. Elthaneos gave me a wink.

"I shall head to the coast to greet the fishermen on the shore. I will help haul their catches. Perhaps a pearl for you waits among the oysters."

I give him a sly look, for I knew the oysters are aphrodisiacs. I also knew my husband would partake of many.

"I shall hurry home tonight, my love, for the sprites are young and will be napping face down in their puddings before dinner can be finished. I will meet you then." With a big wink of my own, which startled a delighted laugh from my twin soul, I blinked out like a snuffed candle.

Moments later, back in body, I slid on my alluring, soft blue gown. I picked up my tiara and nestled it among my long blonde tresses. It was a shining star of a crown that marked my rank as priestess. Then in a flurry of light and sparkle, I was teleported to the castle's Great Hall.

Opening my eyes expectantly, I was greeted by unthinkable horror. The feasting chamber was wet with blood. A massacre had occurred. I could not believe my eyes, or ears, in the eerie silence.

It was a bloodbath.

The troubadour, so famed for his music and verses, was silent. His throat had been slashed and the gift of his angelic voice ripped from his being. But that was not all.

Stunned, I turned to gaze upon the dais. The other six priests and priestesses, along with myself, were the sum total of the Kingdom of Mythoses' cunningwomen and cunningmen, or spiritual healers. That was the closest the Mythoses society had to a pagan clergy rank. These fellow spiritual students, all in God's favor and all present at the creation of the world, now lay slaughtered. Only myself, and only by the sheer luck of my tardiness, had survived to tell the tale. A shudder rose up my spine as I realized my narrow escape.

A cry tore out of me as I noticed the small bodies strewn about the room. All forty-nine of the newly polished little ones had been torn to pieces. None would be able to be identified.

Lying sated among them, snoring softly, Princess Artoria and Kratos breathed deeply. Blood smeared on their hands and clothes spoiled the beatific smiles upon both their faces.

The unsuspecting guests had literally bled to death,

their sweet energy bodies consumed by that dark couple. This draining of their subtle bodies had not allowed the victims to merge within the electromagnetic grids of the Earth Mother. Worst of all, their names and stories could not then be entered into the crystalline grid. Their stories might never be told.

So, I thought to myself, *the eternal flames have all been snuffed. Their souls and bodies exist no more. Truly Artoria is a formidable princess and a terrifying foe.* I telepathically reached for Elthaneos, who absorbed the horror and acted quickly.

The question that remained was this: *where were Princess Artoria's parents?*

Where were our queen and king?

A PRINCESS GONE MAD

Queen Boudica stayed up long into the night, poring over the ancient scrolls written by this "Elanhandra." Boudica needed more insight into the how and why of the destruction of the Kingdom of Mythoses. Rubbing her tired eyes, she continued…

Princess Artoria had been born from a long line of true pagan queens. But in her hurry to ascend the throne and unseat her adoptive parents, the sovereigns who stood in her way, she had made several agreements with the Unseelie king.

Unseelie derived from the old languages, meaning "the unholy." Their counterparts, and sworn enemies, were the *Seelie*. The Seelie Fae were considered both holy and full of light energy. Both the Seelie and the Unseelie had kingdoms far below in the Earth. The Seelie courts glimmered in gold. The Unseelie locked up their gold, preferring to live in darkness.

The Unseelie court was made up of evilly mischievous faeries. No offense was required to have them war against you. Thus these dark imps had enjoyed the bloodletting the ambitious Princess Artoria had requested. They had slain the participants of the royal feast, leaving the carcasses for Artoria and Kratos to devour. All it had required was payment in gold and jewels, and the kingdom had plenty of both.

Artoria's earlier promise of gold and jewels had been enough for the Unseelie king to send an assassin squad to the unsuspecting king and queen of the Kingdom of Mythoses. All faeries dearly love the glittery.

A beautiful apple, poisoned with ricin, had been placed within the queen's favorite fruit basket. Ricin was a deadly poison of the castor bean, an otherwise well-appreciated healing plant. All the elemental beings knew the sweetest nectars, the gentlest healing, and rarest poisons in the plant kingdom. Indeed, the Unseelie king had laughed aloud, amused over his simple murder plot.

Delighted by the unusually bright and shiny apple, the queen had offered the first bite to her true love, the king. She had then licked the maverick juices from his lips and chin. They froze, eyes locked.

In moments, the royal couple had fallen dead upon the floor of their bedchamber. Reflected in their shared gaze was their love for one another, confusion over their dying, and helpless horror. Indifferent, Princess Artoria had hidden in the shadows and calmly watched her parents die.

The queen and king had been unaware of the Unseelie lineage running through the veins of their beautiful adopted daughter's blood. Her tainted blood ran to the darkness. Her greed had caused their early deaths.

In the aftermath, no one suspected the royal deaths were anything but a suicide pact. The Kingdom of Mythoses had never experienced a betrayal or tragedy among all its beauty. Everyone agreed the queen and king had surely chosen to ascend in their evolution together. Whatever the private reasons for the royal suicides, the people now looked to Artoria to ascend to the throne.

All the people of the kingdom wanted to immediately crown Princess Artoria their new queen. There was no suggestion of a formal investigative tribunal, and no objections. There were also no holy court advisors left alive to stop her, except me, Elanhandra. I protested, but none would listen. Upon Princess Artoria's insistence, a coronation and her royal wedding were being planned with all haste.

Only Elthaneos and I stood opposed to crowning Princess Artoria our new queen. The deaths of the royal couple could perhaps be argued as fate. However, the massacre of the music maker, the holy ones, and the innocent children was a horror we would not let escape justice.

****

It was the smug Princess Artoria herself, standing on the curved stairway of the castle, who had done herself in. She was talking to herself, as those possessed with madness often did. She was congratulating herself for the double murders of her loving parents. She grinned as she recounted out loud the shocked expression of the troubadour as Kratos had ripped open his throat. She laughed, remembering the crazed panic of the wee ones, unable to understand death's cruel joke. She applauded herself for ripping out the hearts of the holy ones with her bare hands, and argued with herself about the need to still go after me, Elanhandra.

"Maybe I will kill her," she said out loud, "just for sport and pleasure."

Artoria thought I was the only one who could become a problem for her. I, who was supposed to have died with the others but had arrived late. In their madness, the princess and her consort could wait no longer. The bloodlust of sunset had been upon them. Thus it was that I had stumbled into the aftermath of the blood-letting and found the slaked couple sound asleep. Princess Artoria rightfully feared me, but her mistake was thinking I was her only threat.

Humming and mumbling to herself in a merry way, the soon-to-be-queen Artoria descended the back stairs into the kitchen. As she reached the bottom stair and stepped into the warmth of the baking ovens, Princess Artoria was faced with Elthaneos, dressed in elven armor. His heritage ran to both the holy hosts of Heaven and the golden courts of the Seelie, with a touch of human blood in the mix. The shining Seelie throne was held for him should he ever forsake his human instincts, which the Seelie believed made one weak, to become king. The elven kingdoms, who adored Elthaneos, were in agreement.

Behind him stood a clan of local men, among them the fishers and farmers who had previously feared the princess. But now, in solidarity, anger on their faces, they stood as one and faced the suddenly uncertain Artoria. The bakers and women of the kitchen stood silently back, all eyes locked upon the princess.

The kitchen had been particularly busy, preparing for the hastily planned crowning of their new queen and the celebration to follow. Princess Artoria had been unaware, in her madness, that her conversation with herself on the stairwell had echoed down the stone companionway and been heard by the kitchen workers. Alarmed, a young helper had been sent to fetch Elthaneos. He had hurried to intercept the deranged princess and stop her coronation.

The princess was easily captured, taken in bewilderment and magnetically imprisoned deep within the underground cave systems of the island. Kratos, banished god of war, murderer of his own royal family-to-be, was called by King Zeus back to Mount Olympus.

There his siblings Nike, meaning "victory," Bia, "great

force," and Zelus, the god of zeal, sat as judge and jury. The verdict was swift.

Kratos was forgiven all his actions, which were blamed on the archetypical energies inherent in a war god. Kratos suffered no punishment, which had been King Zeus's desire for his wicked but beloved son.

But King Zeus, in his despair over the many royal sprite deaths, made it his will, and his command, that the sea god should rise and drown the sorrows and secrets of the Kingdom of Mythoses from both time and history. King Neptune did as he was bid, and the favored isle was no more. A few were allowed to escape to the mainland to keep the story and the prophecy of resurrection alive.

In the aftermath, Elthaneos and I spent long moments in human time deliberating with the great King Zeus. In exchange for the ultimate sacrifices offered by the slaughtered innocents, and for all of the Kingdom of Mythoses's beings, human and otherwise, King Zeus, as a portal keeper to the divine Heavens, was persuaded to let loose upon the Earth the seven golden virtues. In exchange, mortals would have to redeem themselves by righting the wrongs of Mythoses in order to have a chance of peace and love on Earth.

It was agreed the heavenly virtues would flood the remaining Middle Earth and help humans to discern. If using their free will to make choices more wisely, it was hoped humanity could prevail against the gathering dark and the netherworld kingdoms of the Unseelie. That was why a handful of the doomed people had been allowed to escape by boat. They were charged with keeping the knowledge of King Zeus's promises alive.

King Zeus further declared that if the descendants of

the true royal lineage could prove themselves worthy once
again to mount the throne, the Kingdom of Mythoses
would rise from the ocean floor and prosper in the world.
It had been rumored that the murdered king had sired a
child before his marriage to the queen. That unknown
child was the only slim hope remaining for the restoration
of Eden on Earth.

In the centuries that followed, Elthaneos and I were
permitted to recover from the demise of our Mythoses
home in grace, atop Olympus. There we nestled into the
quiet mercy of the gods.

THE QUEST OF THE TRINITY BEGINS

Back in the now, the dawn was brightening. Aurora, Skye, and Elandra—along with their royal steeds—could barely contain themselves, all of them eager to be away. The trumpets sounded. The baying of hounds followed. The birds got quiet, and the world held its breath.

Queen Boudica, having spent all night reading the history of the vanished Kingdom of Mythoses in the tattered scrolls, looked pinched and tired. She was also resolute.

"Princess Aurora," proclaimed Queen Boudica, "you go forth as my general, my agent, and my victor in our battle between heavenly light and dark. You are the last of your lineage. Your bloodline, through you, must prove itself compassionate, clever and even discerning. This proof is needed not only for both the human world and Seelie golden court, but also to win the blessings of all the goddesses and gods. You must prove yourself worthy of your crown, your future king and the people over whom you shall rule. If you succeed, Mythoses will be restored better than ever and your lineage shall prevail throughout time. You shall be judged harshly. Do not disappoint me."

Aurora bowed her head.

"Skye, you are of the faery bloodlines of Light. You shall use your tracking and healing skills, and your magic, to protect your small trinity of warriors. The earth and stars shall be your wisdom guides. Do not fail to listen for you, too, shall face challenges. Do not fail to obey the greater powers the golden light draws to you, though your journey may be in darkness."

Skye nodded, excited to be off on their adventure.

"Lastly, my dear Elandra, both human and celestial. You bring compassion great enough to match the warrior skills of death you have all trained for. You shall lead the battles that must be fought, but your path has been blinded by your doubt in God. Heaven will support you. Choose wisely. Choose from your heart."

Elandra also bowed her head, wondering why she felt a bit peeved. *Why lead with your heart when you have a clever mind?*

The three light warriors, reins still in hand, dropped to bended knee. Heads bowed in earnest they swore fealty to the light of God, and to their kingdom and its queen. Elandra crossed her fingers behind her back to purge this partial lie. All was well except her relationship with this supreme God Source they all spoke of. She doubted he had her back.

"Rise and mount!" cried Corban, wizard and advisor of the royal court.

"Elandra," cautioned Queen Boudica quietly, "you shall be mortally challenged upon this journey. I give you this amulet. It shall light your way. It is also a smoky mirror reflection. In it you will see many strange happenings. Question everything. Call for me through the amulet if you feel you have lost the way."

The queen slipped the stone and chain into Elandra's hands as they clasped in farewell. Elandra looked deeply into the queen's eyes. Elandra loved her monarch, who was fair and judicious, whole of heart, and filled with fun. Elandra longed to kiss her cheeks adieu, but protocol would not allow.

The queen's gaze held a knowing smile. "Yes,

daughter, I know," she whispered.

Elandra felt hugged.

Turning in their soft-soled boots, the three friends, warriors of the kingdom of Light, mounted. They were as eager as their snorting beasts to get started.

Soon the trio was swallowed up by the ancient forest. The pounding of hooves faded away, the dust settled, and the warriors were gone. Still Queen Boudica stood gazing after them.

"Corban," she whispered softly, "all hope for this kingdom, perhaps the light in this world, depends on them. Have I done the right thing? Did I train them long and hard enough? Can you foretell the future?"

"All is unknown, my queen. It is truly all in Heaven and God's hands now."

Queen Boudica sighed. "Do you understand to where they ride? Their true destination is to the Edge of the World. That is where I have sent them, although they do not yet know it. There is no other way but should they tumble, there is no saving them. Today, they have ridden out in pure faith. Faith in their steeds, themselves and each other. Faith in God. That shall all be tested."

"God help them." Corban looked troubled.

"Yes, I am fairly confident He shall."

The queen was trying not to read anything into the massive gathering of dark clouds that had begun to obscure the sun.

SADDLE SORE

Elandra's Journal

Day Three: The world is alive! Our adventure has begun and life could not be better.

Day Five: Getting a little saddle sore. Supplies getting lower. Dark skies threaten in the west.

Day Seven: Stupid rain. Too wet for a fire. Hunting and gathering is now our food going forward.

Day Sixteen: It is irritating to me that Skye sings and whistles nonstop. Rory has a foul mouth to go with her hot temper.

Day Seventeen: We have ridden out of the known territories. Our map is useless to us now. We look for moss on the north side of the trees but are in dense forest. It is always wet and chilly. Moss grows everywhere! There is no path that I can see, although Skye, with her faery sight, seems to see which way to go, even when Rory and I cannot.

Day Nineteen: I am peeved about everything. The trip has been boring and we have been squabbling. We don't even know where we are going or what we need to do. Why didn't anyone better explain it all? Why did no one tell us a quest is no real fun?

****

"Oh, please!" Aurora begged. "Can't we dismount and tarry awhile? I need to stretch out my legs in a run, maybe climb a tree for sport." Aurora was indeed keeping within her large cat energy.

Skye reined in her horse, leaning lower to murmur into the great beast's ear. The horse gave a loud huff and rolled its eyes toward Aurora. With a gentle stroking to her mount's neck, a laughing Skye floated from her saddle. Elandra thought she had fluttered out on nearly invisible wings but that may have been a trick of the dappled forest sunlight.

With a silent groan Elandra reined in her steed. Both of them felt travel weary. Elandra slid ungracefully to the ground.

"I am going to find a stream," she announced to the other two. "My horse and I want a long, cool drink of water. For my own self, I want a long bath in fresh water."

"Not only for your own self," muttered Aurora, wrinkling her nose. Skye's tinkling laughter broke the tense mood and avoided the quarrel that might have ensued.

"You are a little ripe yourself, dear friend," Skye said of Aurora. Skye herself seemed to be able to shimmer herself clean with faery radiance. Her temperament was usually merry. When Skye was simply placid, the others understood her to be in her foulest temper.

Aurora and her mount seemed to snort in unison. She leapt to the ground. That was the only way to describe her dismount. In a flash, Aurora was away and loping through the tress. In an instant, the athletic woman had disappeared.

25

"Go. Go!" Skye gestured to Elandra. "It is safe to forage in these woods. I will gather the edible barks, leaves, and flowers. Perhaps I will find some berries." Skye seemed delighted by these possibilities. Elandra's stomach, however, wanted to rebel.

Aurora was the huntress. She kept them in roasted rabbit or squirrel when she could. Elandra found she was wishing for puddings and pie and regretted how soft her appetites had grown in Queen Boudica's beautiful courts.

Using the branch she had taken up as a walking stick, Elandra pushed cautiously into the solitude of the trees. She respected all of nature. She would never be unnecessarily wasteful or forceful. She also knew Mother Earth could fight back and generally won.

Stepping deeper into the foliage all was quiet as the song birds grew still. Not even the smallest of salamanders crunched in the dead leaves of the underbrush. Elandra stopped to listen. She, too, held her breath.

Faintly, she thought she could hear the bubbling rhythm of a gently running waterway. Drawn forward, senses alert, a great thirst guiding her, Elandra stepped beyond a mighty rowan tree. There she got her first glimpse of her precious water.

A picturesque little river, only slightly more forceful than a creek, lazily snaked its way through the forest. The banks were lush with green growth. As she neared the bank, Elandra heard the soft plopping sounds that indicated the presence of several small frogs.

Gratefully, Elandra dropped to both knees. She mumbled a prayer of thanksgiving and lowered her face to the cool current. She drank deeply. Then she rubbed her dirt-coated hands in the water. Finally, she drew handfuls of cold water up and over her head and face. Tired and dusty from the journey, the refreshing water cooled her body and lifted her spirits.

Elandra was having a perfect moment.

Perfect, that is, until she heard what sounded like a large flutter followed by footsteps and quiet laughter.

Water streaming from her face, Elandra hastily wiped her eyes and drew her dagger. She was deadly in a fight so she was annoyed with herself that she had let her defenses drop. To kill with a dagger meant you had to allow your enemy within easy reach. Something Elandra preferred not to do.

Foolish! She berated herself as her eyes scanned left and right.

"Do put that toothpick away. So like mortals to want to play at soldiering when it's much easier to all get along." A sigh followed this pronouncement.

Elandra focused forward and gasped. Slightly above the creek, in a softly glowing halo of light, hovered an ethereal woman figure of light. Beauty was obviously her weapon of choice. She had a killer smile.

Not moving her eyes, Elandra rose to her feet. Her dagger was in her left hand. Her right hand was now on the hilt of her sword. She was ready to pull it and strike.

The shining figure giggled. The sound perplexed Elandra, and did nothing to soothe her suspicions.

"Who are you? What are you about?" she demanded.

The glowing globe of light floated closer. Upon reaching the bank, the woman placed her shimmering slipper-clad feet on the earth. At that connection she seemed to grow more solid, more substantial. Elandra noted the birds had begun to sing again. Small voles and ferrets were reappearing from their hidden spaces. Even the breeze sighed through the trees. Elandra balanced on the tips of her toes, ready to strike.

"Hello, dear one. I am Queen Celestia. I am here, Elandra, at the behest of Heaven to befriend you."

Celestia's voice was pure liquid silver. Her lilting tones were musical, and Elandra could feel the vibrations course through her body.

Conversely, Celestia could easily see how the colors in Elandra's sacred energy system lit up. She knew the small and doomed mortal could feel her resonance. She was enthused about helping to teach this young fighter about love and forgiveness but feared she would be unable to change Elandra's fate.

Stepping closer, the ethereal Celestia came face-to-face with Elandra.

The dagger, held within easy reach of this intruder, had been forgotten. Elandra was spellbound by this being's beauty. Not simply drawn in through a physical or sensual way—although there was that. She literally felt her heart light up with warmth.

Elandra, an orphan all her life, guessed this was what true love felt like. She then wondered where that thought had come from. Queen Celestia's smile grew bigger.

"I am known as an Earth angel. I am also currently queen of all the angels in Heaven. They do my bidding, as I do God's." The queen tilted her head and looked intently at Elandra.

"I am several vibrational levels below those who always remain in Heaven so that I may interact with humans. It must be so. Heaven and Earth are joined as one, but not yet so with all Earth's creatures.

"That means I am many vibrations higher than most Earth beings, especially humans. I am accused of being too sensitive in what can be a highly insensitive earth world. I often feel like a stranger among people when I must visit your villages, hovels, and the courts of mankind. But it does give me a unique, holographic perspective in a world too busy to clearly see what it is about. I volunteered to come down to Earth and help you out."

Elandra knew she was still staring at the radiant figure, but she could not seem to stop.

"What do you mean sent from Heaven?"

"The mission of you and your brave friends has been well noticed in the Kingdom of God. Some are wagering heavily on the outcome. As for myself, I have been assigned to aid and guide you, as you will allow, in an effort to promote your heroic success. I am a queen, yes, but also your humble guide and friend, if you will allow. You may, informally, refer to me as Celestia. We shall be together for a very long time, I am quite sure.

"Should you succeed in placing Aurora upon her throne, her actions as queen will birth great blessings to all of Earth. Prophecy will be fulfilled and the primordial Queen of Love, who has waited a long, long time, will have her chance to bring peace to all. Thus both God and Earth Mother are convinced it would not hurt to offer aid along the way."

"But?" queried Elandra. She could sense Celestia was leaving something unsaid.

"There is the small matter of how skeptical you are of God and all that resonates with God in his universes."

Elandra scoffed. "I have no need of a god." She felt bile rising and turned her head to spit the bitterness from her tongue. That bitterness lived deep within her heart.

"No, certainly not," agreed Queen Celestia. "You have as much goddess or god in you as anyone. But I refer to my God, the one with the capital G. The One. The true divine Source energy. Him, you do have need of. And he is very much filled with unconditional love for you."

Elandra narrowed her eyes. She had endured a difficult and unsupported life. That she now had skills and cunning enough and had been taken under the tutelage of Queen Boudica was an amazing outcome. One she believed she owned all the credit for.

"King Zeus is not a father of love," Elandra said. "He is a father of lovers." Elandra nearly spat again.

The regal Celestia laughed her sparkling laughter. The day brightened, and Elandra felt she was not immune to this woman's joy.

"I do not mean your King Zeus, the god known to man. I mean the one true God. The one forgotten by humans as they recklessly work their way into a deeper separation from the Truth. The true God of many names. Think of him as the gods' God." Celestia winked.

Elandra was certain she heard muted bells ringing and a chorus of quiet laughter. She looked around but saw no one else.

Still cautious, Elandra critically eyed the celestial intruder.

"You are not dressed for a quest. You have no weapons and no horse or cart that I can see. It is not possible for you to join us."

At this, Elandra felt a pang she recognized as instant regret.

The Earth angel's tinkling laugh rang out again.

"Dearest Elandra. I have already joined! I am a part of you, as is God, as is all."

"We will see about that," Elandra snapped. She felt irritated at this stranger's presumptions.

"Yes, we will. Indeed we will." Queen Celestia smiled as she faded from sight.

****

"Are you sure you were not bewitched by a water witch?" Aurora was concerned. Skye was checking Elandra's energy body for spells, sigils, and other energetic intrusions—magicks that could be used to control another's life and bind their free will choice.

Elandra once again found she was irritated. Perhaps she was more tired than she realized.

"No. I tell you, it all happened exactly as I said. I was neither asleep and dreaming nor partaking of leaves and berries that would cause me hallucinations."

Skye considered what Elandra had described.

"Certainly, Earth angels are known to us Seelie. Legend has it there are some but not many. This is indeed an indication of good graces and victory for our journey's outcome."

The women had decided to camp the night by the riverside. They ate fish roasted in leaves over hot rocks. Skye crushed berries into a passable wine. All three felt the need for fortification.

That night, the small group slept deeply. Dreamlessly. No predator stalked them. No weather cursed them. No aches or pains caused restlessness.

They did not realize their little encampment was being held in a glowing sphere of golden light as the ethereal Queen Celestia watched silently over them.

31

THE DISCOVERY

The terrain grew denser and crueler as the trinity of warriors slogged forward through the days. Elandra had given up keeping her journal. It was too dreary. She had tossed it into the smoldering embers of this morning's fire.

Good riddance! She had felt a little lighter and in better spirits watching her grumbly complaints burn to ashes.

Skye and Aurora grew uncertain of their direction, but Elandra, prodded by Celestia, guided them daily and kept them on a path of sorts. As the other two could not see Celestia, this sudden prowess of Elandra's puzzled Skye. Aurora was too grateful to care.

The horses were quick to follow the gentle urgings from Elandra. This allowed them to bypass boggy spots and hillsides with shale so loose a horse could easily falter. To slide on such a treacherous surface would feel like many piercing daggers. Likewise, the bogs could easily claim a horse and rider with no hope of escape.

Despite Elandra's careful route, often enough, the wet ground still made sucking sounds beneath the steeds. Their constant proximity to peril was inescapable. The women were dirty, weary, and becoming disheartened.

Queen Celestia was doing all she could to pull them miraculously forward. They were truly in need of fortification, to a much greater degree than wine could ever provide. Celestia had a destination in mind that she did not think these three humans would like, but she knew it was important they get there. This quest was about much more than Aurora's throne.

She also knew these three women who felt like misfits

in the human world truly were rarities.

Skye's faery blood had become mixed with human. Her Fae lineage was of the golden faeries, the benevolent and always joyful Seelie. Yet even among them, some were home bodies, preferring the underground high courts of the Seelie. Others were born with a wanderlust that was insatiable. They traveled above ground and reported back to their queen. Skye was from this latter group, and thus had human blood entered her magickal bloodline.

Aurora practiced therianthropy, a not-so-mythical ability to metamorphose into animals. When needed, Aurora could call the archetypical energies of a lioness to her so strongly that she could manifest into the great beast at will. Most knew her as a werecat, or female shape-shifter, but the truth was she was most often human, with a ferocious and snarly aspect that often got her in trouble.

But Elandra was the puzzle Celestia had been sent to solve. Born of a human mother, fathered by a lesser god who had seduced the young maiden, Elandra could potentiate a conduit between Heaven and man that would greatly shift human evolution. The biggest problem was Elandra needed to know and believe in God as much as God knew and believed in her. Queen Celestia had her work cut out for her.

Just after Elandra's birthing, her mother had slept while Elandra's maternal grandfather wrapped the scrawny infant in rough cloth and old linens. When the mother awoke, she learned that her daughter was gone. Elandra's mother died of a broken heart soon after.

The minor god that was Elandra's father was so bereft at these events, he turned inward. He refused to shine his Light or to remain the conduit he had been between

Heaven and Earth in service to God. It was now up to Elandra to heal this rift in her lineage.

Placed with passing gypsies, Elandra had not fared well. As she grew, it was hard not to notice something was odd about the petite child. She was pretty enough. Also she was fairly well schooled in survival, if not in scholarly matters. Elandra was even polite and dutiful enough. She had found out early in life about the heavy-handedness that followed her acts of rebellion.

Her oddness was something greater. This "something" marked her as different and made people uncomfortable. It was this strangeness that made others wary of her.

The gypsies could not afford to be noticed as they played their shell games and bait-and-switch and applied the seductions that were a way of life on the road. They could not afford for anyone to remember the odd blue-eyed, blonde-haired child. Too many questions would be asked as to how she had come to live among the swarthy-skinned, deep-eyed people of the traveling caravan. So far, they had hidden her in the caravan wagons, doors closed and windows made opaque by fluttering veils when around any towns or settlements. As the child grew, the gypsies felt a decision must finally be made.

Thus Elandra, just a small child of five, was left behind at the gates to Queen Boudica's castle.

Just outside the gates to the castle, Elandra's gypsy family had ordered the five-year-old to sneak into the marketplace to steal anything she could. She gingerly made her way forward, all alone and covered in a small, hooded cape. By the time she returned, the gypsy family had quickly broken camp and moved off in her absence.

Bewildered, a frightened Elandra huddled into herself

at the side of the gate, a pilfered loaf of bread her only possession. She cried herself to sleep. At dusk, just before the closing of the heavy gated portal, a merchant, unknowingly guided by Queen Celestia, found the child.

The kind-hearted man lifted the sleeping child into his cart. He took her into the safety of the castle walls. He knew the child would never survive the harshness of the nighttime growlers, beasts and humans alike.

The merchant's plump, jolly wife cleaned up the urchin and presented her the next day at afternoon tea with the other high-society women. Her story—*this amazing find*—was the talk of the town. None of the women could resist repeating the mysterious tale. The appearance of this golden-haired child was indeed a mystery among the kingdom's people.

Eventually, the queen's court heard the whispering. Celestia intervened again. Queen Boudica ordered the child to be brought before her.

Staring deeply into the child's bright blue eyes, the queen believed she had glimpsed a soul so shining as to be prophetic. She commanded that Elandra should be raised with Skye and Aurora, other foundlings brought to her attention in similar ways. The queen did not realize that Celestia was prodding her to tempt fate, but tempt fate she did.

Queen Boudica brought the three young children together and blended them into a family closer than any they had ever known. She decreed they should be trained and prepared for any adventure. The queen could not know each child's specific purpose, but she was wise, fierce, and believed in being ready.

Eventually, Queen Celestia had disclosed, through old

scrolls, Aurora's royal claim on the ancient, bedeviled kingdom of Mythoses. Folklore told the rest of the tales.

Queen Boudica then understood the importance of this trinity of girls.

TRANCE DANCE

Elandra was snapped out of her musings by a cry and a groan. Skye had dismounted to lead her faltering horse forward. While looking backward, telepathically encouraging her mount, she failed to see the slick lichen on the rocky ground. Despite her wings, Skye slipped and badly twisted her ankle. They would journey no further today.

Aurora, the huntress, looked around. They were in a defensible grove. The sunshine was upon them, although huge trees reached for the sky in a circle around them. She approved of the site for setting up camp for the night.

Elandra agreed. Her warrior senses were at peace. She did feel something magical charge the air. She glanced over among the pines, and there Queen Celestia glowed like a star. She gave Elandra a nod of approval. Elandra shot her back a small smile and a faint nod of her own. Despite herself, the presence of Celestia was calming to Elandra. She was actually feeling excited about this unexpected respite.

Skye was in too much pain to care. She had no quarrel with where they spent the night. She herself was a renowned healer and her faery magicks could heal quickly. Just one more reason the others were happy she was with them. She needed only a place to rest and focus to heal her aches and pains.

In her distraction, Skye failed to notice the soft twilight glow under the dark hangings of the bushes and trees. Had she been paying attention, she would have realized they were encamped in a faery ring. She would have made sure to investigate whether this was a stronghold of her Seelie brethren or had they stumbled upon holdings of the mischievous Unseelie.

It was always wise to avoid her dark cousins.

****

As Skye slept, covered in a blanket of flower petals and her healing in full blossom, the Moon Mother looked down and saw the sleeping faery.

Skye was dancing among the astral planes, as faeries are wont to do in the very few hours of sleep a faery body requires, even when healing. It was here, while the fiddles played at a hypnotic pace, that the Seelie whirled in feverish trance, including ecstatic dance. This was the dance style of most magickal people. Human dance paled in comparison.

As Skye swirled and laughed, a bright beam of moonlight opened up a path before her dancing feet. No stranger to the strangeness between the worlds, Skye immediately skipped her way forward.

When the path ended, Skye was immediately startled. She dropped and held a deep curtsy.

"Arise, my child. Arise."

Skye obeyed the pleasantly low voice. Light and sound began to move again, and Elbereth, queen of benevolence, stepped fully into view.

Queen Elbereth had long ruled the moon and the stars. She was the one who could send heavenly light into the dark and keep night predators at bay.

"Hello, Good Mother," said Skye in formal elven tongue. "To what do I owe such an honor?"

"Good Mother" was considered the ultimate title of respect and honor. It was appropriate among the magickal beings as they often crossed in time and space, making some formal titles, such as aunt or even "grand" a bit confusing. Unlike humans, they understood that Father Time actually ran in a circular, not linear, way.

Skye stood at polite attention. It was a rare and special moment when Queen Elbereth showed herself.

"My dear faery, I have come to give you both counsel and warning. You travel to put the werecat back upon the throne. It is noble and good. But your part in this journey is larger and sacred to your people. You must seek the kumari, or princess, Devi. She is a primordial energy. She has now been called into human-like form. She presents as prepubescent girl energy, immature, but not beyond her years."

Princess Devi was a divine female, an ancient archetypical energy. Archetypical energies such as the virtues or other agents of Heaven and hell were capable of being pulled into the third dimension of Earth as reality. They presented as real and solid beings. As such, she was born primordial queen of all the plant devas, even though forever captured in the joyous energy of her girlhood form

"The Princess Devi is destined to become the most important queen for this world. But this cannot be so, under orders from King Zeus and due to his agreements with both God and the humans. Not until Mythoses is restored as a new kingdom may the kumari ascend to Queen of Love and Peace on Earth. Meanwhile, Princess Devi has been under the ancient tutelage of Yada, preparing for all your futures."

Skye could not help but be visibly startled. Yada was a long-forgotten, pre-religious practice of learning to know, to love, and to be. Acolytes of Yada stood in the highest grace from God. In the higher realms, Yada was believed to be the mystical recipe for all beings wishing to restore Heaven on Earth.

As part faery, Skye understood that every plant and flower, each mustard seed, had a deva. It was a life force, a being who was the soul of the flora. The faery lore said the fabled Kumari Devi, who was birthed primordial queen of all the devas and would someday arise to be Queen Devi, always brought joy and laughter to all her plant people. Their kingdom was a happy one. They lived in service, providing Mother Earth herself with food, medicines, and beauty. Not to mention the air!

Without the kumari's Kingdom of All Flora, the Earth and her other children would have no air to breathe. Life could not be without these happy souls. The kumari's devas also maintained the crystal, electric, and magnetic grids of Earth. This Kumari would one day expand her reign to encompass also being the Queen of Love and Peace on Earth, should this quest succeed.

"Yes, Good Mother, I know the lore. What do you wish of me?"

If the kumari is to be a future queen, but she is already queen of all the devas, what added power is she in lineage for? How powerful could one queen be?

Skye was struggling to understand the nuances of what she was hearing. Local Fae folklore did not address the event of the primordial kumari's ascension, or her double crowning.

"The queen of all devas is prophesized to also become the queen of love and peace on this planet. As such, she will use the planet's root systems and crystalline grids to send the higher vibrations of love, joy, peace, and compassion out to all the beings of Earth. Her stone people, the crystal children, the creepy crawlers, winged beings, all the furred and four-leggeds, as well as the elemental beings and humans, will all be effected. This is critical to Earth's ascension and also her survival.

"Protect your impetuous Aurora. She is mighty and fierce but tends to forget herself. She must be successful. With the crown upon Aurora's head, great gifts from all the kingdoms and blessings from all the heavens can be bestowed. Once this occurs our kumari may ascend further in her own destiny. Princess Devi will be allowed to take her rightful and long-awaited place as the Queen of Love in this universe.

"She will then be allowed to send her effervescent joy and God's unconditional love through the Earth's crystalline grids, long guarded by the Fae. Every creature, large and small, will be uplifted. All will be awash in a resonance of holy love. Then, and only then, can there be true peace on Earth."

Skye shivered with delight. The queen of benevolence was prophesizing the rise in Earth's third dimensionality to a place high enough for all the kingdoms to finally be reunited. The Fae had long whispered this tale. So long, in fact, that many had begun to doubt its veracity.

"As goes Aurora's quest, so goes the kumari's. My gift to you, my beautiful Skye, is fortitude. You shall have courage, but unlike Aurora, you will not be foolhardy. You shall display patience and perseverance.

"Fortitude is a divine virtue, as are patience and perseverance. You are a virtuous, although tainted, blood Seelie. By *tainted*, I mean the peccadillos of human blood also flow within you and must be respected. In some ways,

41

it makes you stronger. You were born virtuous, as were your companions. You all have firm, even habitual, dispositions to do good things. That is what the humans, with their blind eyes and deaf ears, have disliked about the three of you.

"But know this: what and how you do a thing matters. It matters greatly. Very little is needed to upset the harmonics within nature. The human propensity for ever-growing darkness and ill deeds is just such a threat to all balance."

Skye understood. Mother Nature, by her own nature, must be preserved and revered. Without her, the world would literally stop breathing. Skye was reverent, for in her Seelie culture, all life was to be revered.

"Yes, Good Mother. Tell me specifically what I must do, and I promise you, I shall."

"Stay persistent. Remain ethical. Be forewarned, my child, that great emotional depressions, the loss of childlike delight, the marring of the God light in souls, all dim the heart. Then all courage is lost. Despair would uproot your purpose if given the chance. These things are powerful workings of that despicable and insatiable demon Sloth.

"Fortitude is a virtue. She will come forward embodied as a living goddess known to you as Fortitude. She will support you and your trinity. Sloth is an evil. It will come personified as the demon soul it is and try to pit itself against you. To do so, it must attack you through your humanness. Should this ancient demon overcome the virtue of Fortitude, Earth could be lost in a deep darkness for many millenniums. Perhaps lost forever."

Skye told herself to focus on much needed fortitude, so

she could keep the dark at bay. She would have to think about the other heavenly virtues—prudence, justice, temperance, faith, hope, and charity. She wouldn't mind having them along as well.

Skye was still forming her questions for the queen when outside of her own control she sleepily opened her eyes. She had awakened in the peaceful grove, amid the flower petals and gentle snores of her companions. A dozing horse swished its tail.

Skye glanced around. All was safe. Moonlight shone down brightly upon their little camp. The stars twinkled, having overheard the secrets Skye and Queen Elbereth had shared. With a sigh of contentment, Skye mumbled a quick prayer of faith in all the good mothers of the universes and snuggled back down into a dreamless sleep.

The spirit of Fortitude, already embodied as a shimmering feminine light being, was perched on a nearby log, smiling at the sleeping trio.

THE SEELIE QUEEN

Aurora was relieved as the trio left the dense forest behind. She enjoyed the open spaces of the meadows they were now traversing. Game was plentiful, and she felt feline enjoyment in the afternoon sun as it warmed. She fought against the languid feelings the warm delight brought her. She sighed with contentment. *I am happy there is bigger game. I am quite tired of rodents and fish for dinner.*

Skye thought Aurora looked like she was purring. For herself, she was equally at home in forest or field. She remained content, even optimistic, humming aloud her bright, lively tunes.

Elandra felt more wary. She disliked the openness of their position. Should a storm or attack arise, there was no immediate shelter. She kept alert, but day after day the drowsy summer meadow stayed peaceful and friendly.

On the eighth sunrise of nonstop traveling through vast open meadow spaces, as the early-morning glow of dawn was replacing the nighttime of glowing protections the queens Celestia and Elbereth had blessed them with, the women were again breaking camp.

"Why so early?" grumbled Aurora, who often paced restlessly in her lioness form throughout the night. "I have been far and wide. All is quiet."

Except for the dying shrieks of that hartebeest, thought Elandra sourly. Aurora had failed to bring the young antelope down with one try. The wounded animal had screamed several times before being quieted by the fatal slashes of Aurora's sharp claws and teeth.

44

Elandra accepted the carnivorous needs of her good friend, but she was queasy at the sounds of death. She hoped they would never be required to place their own blood into the ground as penance. Still, her stomach did prefer a strip of roasted meat over bugs and bark.

Skye, who best understood it was a great balance, was unperturbed at the sacrifices it took to feed their small group. She would never take more than was needed and always gave thanks and offering.

"I feel watched." Elandra was petulant. "The trees have eyes and ears, but I do not know what abounds here. Something is coming. I hope if we ride swiftly, we will be gone before it arrives."

Skye and Aurora glanced at each other. They felt no threat, but in truth, it had been Queen Celestia who had roused Elandra and urged them all forward in the dawning light. Her urgency had alarmed Elandra.

As they mounted, Elandra looked for the glowing globe that was Celestia in the sea of grass. The dawn was east, at their backs, but the celestial being was drawing them northwest. Following her guidance was easier than sky-mapping an uncertain route.

As the day warmed, the women struggled free of their elven cloaks. The cloaks were woven of earth tones and hid them well within nature, but Skye and Aurora were hot and dusty, and convinced no threat loomed. Skye often bent down, murmuring words of encouragement to her horse.

Elandra kept a cautious eye out and her sword by her side.

Eventually, on their horizon, a few stone mounds appeared. Elandra decided these were not mirages. A few scraggly trees came to view as they drew closer to the hillocks. This northwest trail had led them toward the highlands. Elandra was relieved.

"Let's push on toward those hillocks with trees. Perhaps we can find a waterway and break early for camp. We are all tired."

Skye's laughter sparkled into the air. "Speak for yourself, lazy one."

She, too, had been awake to witness the dying moans of Aurora's kill and had given reverent thanks to the cycle of all life. She was nonplussed and still well rested.

Aurora announced she could smell water.

"I will fly ahead a wee bit and check for a river or a stream," Skye said. "We can make camp there."

Skye lifted off from her horse and shimmered out of sight. Although her human blood lessened the powers of her faery magicks, short flights and near invisibility were a way of life for her. The Fae had long trusted in these skills to keep them safe above ground.

As Aurora and Elandra plodded forward, Skye's mount fell into step behind them. Her steed was much devoted to Skye, animal-whisperer that she was. In her absence, the horse's instinct drew it into the herd.

A happy shout and a sparkle of fireworks appeared a few clicks ahead. The two warriors kicked their horses into a trot. Skye had found a campsite that suited.

Arriving at the spot, the women gazed at a half-rounded hillock that formed a partial circle, a shelter of sorts. Green trees and fertile grasses seemed to wave them inside. A small tributary from a large river to the north ran nearby.

The meadows they had traversed had been full of small rivulets, but none so deep or swift that they had been stumped. The horses had been able to ford the waters, even laden as they were with the trinity of warriors and all their gear.

Skye was excited. Elandra had assumed unofficial charge. As things were going well, it was hard to protest, but still, Skye felt she had more to contribute. Impetuous Aurora was the one with the real control issues. She could get very snarly, very quickly.

The truth was having great courage and world-class fighting skills would bring out the confidence in anybody. Skye understood there was a thin line between altruism and arrogance. Aurora could be prideful in her certainty. Skye figured that was part of her lioness energy.

Elandra, so used to foraging alone, had a hard time trusting. She tamped down any fears with a confidence that did not always shine out through her eyes.

Skye, more used to large troupes at faery gatherings, was more acquiescent. The Fae had a pretty strict caste system, and Skye was used to being in a comfortable position between leader and follower.

"Why are these great stones set as if serving as table and chairs?" Elandra asked. It perplexed her and made her uneasy. *Who had lived here? Or lived here still?*

"I smell ancient chars from spent fires," added Aurora, sniffing at the air carefully and wondering at the humanoid smells she detected.

"This is a perfect encampment. I am sure *many* have used it along the way." Skye was a little peeved and almost growled out the words. But she restrained herself in time. She felt really pulled to this spot she had chosen and truly wished to stay. She did not want the others to overrule her.

It was hard to protest Skye's logic, and everyone was tired, so the other two reluctantly agreed. They were eager to set up camp in the daylight instead of fumbling around in the dark. Evening grew quicker in these hills than on the flat plains.

As Elandra and Aurora began to unpack the horses, Skye felt drawn to explore the rounded hillock and its surrounding shadows. She perched upon a rock and struggled to regain her natural balance.

She was slightly troubled that the positioning of this boulder near the meandering water might make for a quaint fishing spot for a very large being. The rock she sat upon sent vibrations of slumberous warning. The stone people were friendly to the Fae but never got directly involved in any conflicts.

Skye, feeling chilled, shook herself and drew in the brightest of the waning sunbeams to warm her. She ignored the warnings of the stones.

I have let a dour Elandra prey upon my courage. We have been many moons upon our journey and have never met a potential enemy—not even nature, which can be a dire foe but has been our true love and provided richly for our needs. I just need more time alone in nature, nurturing myself.

Skye smiled. She was melting back into the bliss that was her more natural state.

"Relax, dear one, and meld with me." The voice was soft as a breeze.

Skye perked up and looked around.

Floating up and to the left was a violet ball of light. Skye knew this to be both a benevolent color and a vibration of glory.

"Yes, Good Mother?" Skye was uncertain who was talking to her, but she held no distrust.

The globe shimmered and drew closer. It gently shook into the likeness of a small crone. She stood only about three feet high on her own but continued to hover several feet above the earth.

"I am Sister Phaena, which means 'bright one.' It is truly my pleasure to be a messenger from the realm of Queen Elbereth."

Skye remembered her encounter with the queen. The memory sent a delighted shiver up her spine.

"Yes, my sister. You are most welcome here." Skye floated up off the rock, the better to curtsy to her visitor from the stars.

"I am here to warn you. There are dangerous steps ahead, my young sister. You must heed yourself. Remember your gift of fortitude. Make your faery blood proud. Trouble is close, and you must victor over your own self."

Skye was puzzled. Her human side felt annoyed. She was being lectured, yet hadn't she always upheld herself as the epitome of Fae grace?

"What kind of trouble do you mean, good sister?"

"That is all I have been permitted to reveal. Harken my words, favored daughter of the Seelie queen. Your challenge is upon you!"

With that, the tiny being winked away.

Skye blinked. Had she not been of magickal lineage herself, she would not have believed her encounter. She fluttered back to the ground and rejoined the others. Her placid silence was enough to have the others wondering about her foul mood. Both felt curious but were too inhibited to ask.

Without the gay song and dance Skye always brought 'round the fire, everyone grew quiet. Elandra excused herself to her bedroll. She was hoping the meditative silence would bring her great insight.

Aurora, still full from last night's successful hunt, escaped the moroseness by prowling down to the stream. There she bathed and slaked her thirst. Moments after her return, she was sprawled fast asleep upon her bedroll.

It was then that the L'annawnshe, the royal underworld faeries, appeared. Skye bolted upright and then sank to the ground, her forehead touching earth.

"My queen," Skye exclaimed, for it was indeed the Seelie queen who stood before her. Music piped through the air, and an entourage of glimmering beings stood at a respectful distance.

Seelie queens and kings were always known as the Ones Whose Names Must Not Be Known. Names held great power. Their names could not be said aloud upon pain of death. This was to protect any royal couple from dark magicks, spells, sorcery, and the like. Thus, Seelie royals ruled for many millenniums.

Skye was flabbergasted.

Blessedly happy, the Seelie queen of Earth and Fae ruled both the home-loving and the adventuring good faeries. It was not unusual for the meeker of the dark faeries to try to escape their Unseelie king and seek refuge in the Seelie courts. This queen was famed for her kindness.

"My child, I have been your guide throughout your short life. I sent my sister, Queen Elbereth, to you. She has gifted you Fortitude as a companion and also sent the good

Sister Phaena. Still, we are concerned about your human impetuousness."

Skye would have paled if such a thing were possible of a luminous light being. *Hadn't she been told her human blood was a blessing?*

"And a curse," replied the Seelie queen, easily discerning Skye's thoughts. "Your challenge is first. Your loyalty is not in question, but your heart may betray us all. Be cautious, my daughter, for a slippery slope is long and gets forever steeper. There is no coming back."

The queen leaned in and graced Skye with a kiss to her forehead. With a benign smile, the queen's light faded, taking her royal party with her.

Skye stood uncertainly. *What could possibly be about to befall them?*

TROLL TROUBLE

A hideous loud roar broke the night silence. Then a dull booming began thundering through the ground. The sleeping encampment awoke with a jolt.

The first to leap to her feet, Aurora bounded up a large outcropping of rocks to look around. An enormous troll-ogre hybrid was pounding a lethal-looking club on the ground in anguish.

Noticing the startled movements of the camp, the elemental giant blazed his anger toward the three women. With a roar, he stumbled forward. He would have smashed Aurora to smithereens if she hadn't nimbly leapt aside.

"Flee! Flee!" she called.

Skye was already making for the horses, abandoning their camping gear, as Elandra stood stunned.

Aurora dropped swiftly to Elandra's side and shook her vehemently.

"Get to the horses. Ride! You are our most vulnerable."

It was true. Aurora, in her cat form, could run like the wind. Skye could fly.

Dumbfounded, and for the first time realizing her disadvantage, Elandra broke for the horses. She scooped up her shield and scabbard with the sword she always kept close and kept on running.

The giant sized elemental being, furious at intruders in his summer encampment, plunged after Elandra. The horses neighed in fear but stood their ground. Hooves flashing, the war horses surrounded Elandra, who was trying to mount any one of the moving steeds.

The tight group circled and dodged as the enraged troll-ogre slammed and banged at them. One blow would be enough to crush Elandra. The horses were also at great risk.

Skye circled the hybrid's head, sending bolts of electrical charges at him. Aurora flashed teeth and claws, trying to cut its Achilles tendon and thus cripple the humanoid beast. Then they could escape.

A walloping blow caught Skye's horse. The animal screamed in agony as it was knocked from its feet.

"Aethelwyne. No!"

Skye was enraged. Aethelwyne was the name she had given her horse-brother. It meant "friend" in all the elemental kingdoms.

She flew at the intruder, pelting stones at his face. Blindly, the troll hybrid struck out again, landing a killing blow to the ailing horse.

All time seemed to stop as the agony of the precious steed ran its dying course. The other two horses, greatly spooked, dashed into the night. Aurora and Elandra, spellbound, stood just staring. Skye held her loyal beast's head and sang soft lullabies in the ancient elven tongues of healing. Even her formidable healing skills, however, could not reverse death.

The troll-ogre mixed breed, mollified at the carnage he had caused, moved into the camp. He stomped out the embers of the night's fire and then moved to the women's bedrolls and provisions.

Skye, enraged by her grief for Aethelwyne, drew her sword and marched forward. "Hey! Hey, you! Ugly one. Don't be a pissant!"

"A pissant, is it?" The giant hybrid creature roared.

Aurora looked with alarm at Elandra, who just rolled

her eyes.

"I do the roaring around here!" called Aurora. She bared teeth and fangs and leapt into the fray. She was nothing if not a friend to the end.

Elandra shook her head. *Would they never learn?* With a sigh, she hoisted her shield and sword and followed her friends into battle.

The sacred amulet from Queen Boudica, which Elandra wore on a chain over her heart, began to glow blood red.

****

Queen Boudica, watching through her crystal sphere, sighed. Her trinity of women had failed their first big test.

Kindhearted Skye, in love with all living creatures, was forsaking her Fae disciplines for human revenge. Even more, if Skye, in her pride, had not insisted on taking over the troll-ogre's encampment for the night, all battle could have been avoided. Human blood ran hot, and Skye had fallen victim to its heat.

Boudica watched as with clever fighting skills the women advanced upon their wounded adversary. Through tooth, claw, and blade, they out stung the great elemental until with a final yodel he retreated back into the darkness and vanished. Skye, normally a creature of peace, swore to track and kill him.

Queen Celestia, who had been lighting up the night, let her light dim. Clouds obscured the moon and stars, clear signs of the upset of Queen Elbereth and Sister Phaena. The entire Seelie court was silent as their queen prayed her magicks.

Off in the brush, the bloated, scabby, and stubby demon Sloth, who had ridden in on the angry troll hybrid, held the virtue goddess Fortitude in a cruel grip. Its clawed hand was tight across her mouth.

Fortitude struggled as Sloth sought to abduct her but Skye was unwilling to see or hear her. Skye was feeling defeated. She was unable to be of any help. Sloth dragged Fortitude away by her hair.

In the aftermath of battle and the burial of her dear friend Aethelwyn, Skye continued silent and withdrawn. This was as morose as the Fae could ever be. Aurora and Elandra were worried. Sloth, an expert in causing, and enjoying, great despair, laughed from his hiding place in the deep shadows. Fortitude, feeling momentarily defeated, was slumped despondently by his side.

The burial itself was offered with song, flowers, and blessings for the good afterlife of the noble Aethelwyn. In all the ancient tongues, a somber service was conducted, assisted by all the mourning plant devas. All three warriors wept. Flowers now grew, and always would, in all the colors of the rainbow around the final resting place of this hooved friend to all.

The grieving women turned their thoughts to their own survival.

The other two horses were finally recaptured. Skye could easily have ridden with either companion, but she refused to bond again with another horse. This journey was no longer just fun and games.

Skye wanted revenge.

She alternatively marched and flew while the others trailed passively behind on their mounts. The slim and gentle virtue goddess Hope trailed silently behind, simply wishing to be noticed.

SWEET VENGEANCE

The trinity of friends slogged onward. There didn't seem to be too much to say. Skye brooded, which worried the others. They had come to depend on her lighthearted cheer. The terrain was uneven, and cloudy skies had become the norm.

The gentlest virtue, Hope, had taken up silent and invisible residence among the three, biding her time. She knew things could always get worse before they got better, if allowed to.

Her niece Patience had joined her. Hope was grateful. She always found great potential in the calming presence of the optimistic Patience. Perseverance, sister of Patience, also joined them in time. Fortitude would eventually catch up, but was not currently needed. The Virtue Hope must be accepted before Fortitude could really make any difference. The days dragged on. The three feminine embodied virtues, Hope, Patience and Perseverance dragged on with them.

Patience and Perseverance were the twin daughters of the virtue goddess Prudence. Prudence was known as the grandmother of all the virtues. She reigned with humility and wisdom. The deadly sin of Pride was her biggest foe, one she was always on the alert for. Pride was large, leathery, and horrible to encounter. This demon could suck all humility and kindness out of an unaware human, and enjoy every moment of it.

The demon Pride had made a point of doing a victory dance when Skye's wounded human side had insisted on ignoring wise counsel. She had listened to the whisperings of this nemesis and ignored the sagacity, discipline, and foresight that Prudence had tried to bring her through a council of elite beings, such as Queen Elbereth and Sister Phaena. Light beings that Skye had ultimately ignored. Wrath had now joined Pride in embodiment. Its anger could be felt like a smothering blanket. This crusty red, scaly being was cruel, and its laughter was bitter. Wrath enjoyed causing great harm.

As Skye's anger grew, Hope felt faint. The demon sins howled in delight.

Grandmother Prudence would step in when needed, but for now, she was pleased that Patience and Perseverance were there to cheer up Hope. She knew when Hope was shining; everyone who was paying attention could feel her.

Fortitude, having bitten Sloth's hand nearly off, had escaped the demon's powerful grip and caught up with the trio.

So Aurora and Elandra bided their time. They were not despondent, thanks to Hope and Fortitude, but they were concerned for Skye nonetheless. Her heart had truly hardened.

Skye felt a rare urgency to trek forward, to put more distance between them and the nightmare of Aethelwyn's death. Only the human side of eternal beings could feel such need. She knew she now doubted herself. Aethelwyn had died. She doubted her defense skills. She doubted goodness in this world. For the first time, Skye even doubted the outcome of their journey. She was worn out with grief.

The virtue goddess Faith did not make an appearance. Until Skye could feel Hope's presence, she could never acknowledge Faith.

The sin of Sloth was a little put out that Skye did not wallow more miserably in her grief by slowing down and giving in. Skye was somewhat feeling the presence of the goddess Fortitude, who simply waved Sloth away. But Sloth was happy that the deadly sin Wrath had shown up. Skye had chosen Wrath's whispered advice. She wanted vengeance. Sloth's time here might be up, but things always got interesting when the human lineages gave into to their anger.

Fortitude was keeping a careful eye on Hope. Hope was often fragile, and the strongest of all deadly sins, Pride, had sent his niece Vanity to spy and report back. Vanity could bring out the preening worst in a person or decimate someone's self-confidence. She was trailing around after Skye, but taunting all of them. It was likely Pride and his cohorts could trip up Skye in her humanness once again. The heavenly virtues feared that Skye's crimes could become fatal to this trinity's holy mission.

****

Elandra gathered and stacked wood for a campfire. She still thought she felt unseen eyes upon them, but Queen Celestia was peaceful and that was reassuring. Celestia flicked her wrist, and a shower of sparkles arced from her hand and ignited the stacked kindling. Grateful, Elandra drew in close to the small blaze. The temperatures had turned cooler.

Queen Boudica continued to watch through her crystal ball. The amulet, now returned to its normal golden color, faithfully gave her a bird's-eye view of the trek. Boudica wished she could speak to Elandra. The only way she could was if Elandra first called out to Boudica by name for counsel. Elandra was not clear about this, and had not thought to do so. Boudica sighed, berating herself for not making it clearer on the day the trinity departed that the amulet was a sacred two-way communication device.

After the three shared a light supper, Elandra nestled down in the salvaged remains of her bedroll. Unlike celestial beings, this halfling was susceptible to feeling chilled. As the blankets wrapped around her gradually began to warm her body, Elandra's attention became fuzzy. Eyes half-closed, she barely heard Celestia's telepathic whisper that tomorrow would *bring enough changes and tonight was the time for rest.*

Elandra was too disheartened and tired to even wonder what that might mean.

Once she figured the other two had settled in, a alert Skye finally tossed her blankets aside and donned her cloak. Hesitating briefly, she decided her companions were deeply asleep and would remain so. Then she snuck away.

Aurora opened one eye. She had watched Skye on other nights, tracking the earth and stars. She wasn't sure what exactly Skye was looking for, but the faery's movements were odd enough.

Aurora silently rose and padded off after her faery friend.

****

Since faeries could fly faster than even a great cat could run, it took Aurora a while to locate Skye. Her sensitive nose could smell faery dust, but also something else. That "something" was coppery and sinister.

Aurora bounded to the top of a small stone mesa. Again, she had the eerie feeling that these large stones and boulders had been placed by giant beings for more than just random purposes. Aurora was uneasy.

As she crested the hill, the large cat faltered, slipping back into the red-haired warrior she truly was once again. The smells were too gross for her sensitive cat nose.

The terrible troll-ogre who had attacked the small tribe of friends lay beheaded upon the ground. His bowels had let loose and lay steaming. He had been attacked as he slept on a different mesa of rock. Aurora now realized these rock formations formed beds for large elemental beings. She scowled. *This felt all wrong.*

Skye was wiping maroon-colored blood from her sword onto the sweet grasses, who were weeping. She looked up at a familiar growl.

"Hello, Rory," Skye said indifferently. "I'm finally finished here and good riddance." Then Skye smiled her first real smile since Aethelwyn had fallen.

"Skye, what have you done?" The wild cat in Aurora applauded, but her human side recoiled.

"I have claimed justice!"

"You know Elandra is not going to like this," Aurora cautioned.

"Then we shan't tell her, shall we?" Skye turned her eyes toward the werecat.

Aurora saw something pass through those eyes. Something wickedly human that had momentarily made Skye's clear blue eyes turn murky brown. Her eyes wavered and became bright blue again. Aurora thought maybe Skye had returned to her senses. She hoped so.

She deliberated. "OK, then. I will keep this our violent secret, in the interest of peace."

The two blood hunters sealed their bargain with a solemn handshake, unaware of the oxymoron. Skye could hear the uproarious laughter of the dark Unseelie king rumble through the underground. He was always one to prefer a sacred bonding through bloodletting. This secret pact delighted him.

The stoic Seelie queen of golden courts would not weep, although she wanted to. Her heart feared for her little Skye, who seemed to be losing her way. Fallen Seelie were permanently exiled from her kingdom. There was no other recourse. Skye could be doomed to forever seek refuge in the Unseelie kingdom or risk just simply fading away.

RASHNESS AND REPRIMANDS

Aurora and Skye had just returned to the sanctuary of their campfire when the virtue goddess Prudence strode into the light. Aurora looked surprised, but Skye just sighed, resigned.

There was no preamble or niceties.

"I have been summoned by my daughters, Patience and Perseverance. They tell me I am much needed here. That because of you"—the mother of virtues pointed at Skye—"my goddess sisters Hope and Fortitude, who are trying to help you, have both been taken hostage this time by Wrath and Sloth. You, silly girl, are not to continue making such poor choices."

Mother Prudence snapped her fingers. Like the cowards that they were, Sloth released Fortitude and fled with Vanity. Wrath was tougher, but drooped like a scolded dog, tail between its legs, and bared its teeth. It softly hissed at the newcomer, still gripping Hope and leaning in close towards Skye.

The goddess Hope leapt forward, pulling free from the distracted Wrath's scarred and scaly grasp. She pivoted and kicked the demon in its ample behind. Flatulence was the only sound as Wrath escaped into the night.

With Wrath's retreat, Skye's anger neutralized. Prudence, the great Good Mother, beckoned, and her sister, the virtue goddess Justice, sailed in.

"Hello, Skye." Her voice was pleasant and her countenance was calm. Aurora could not tell if Justice was pleased or displeased.

"I am here, dear faery, not in judgment, for the past is

the past. It is the future I fear for. Going forward means good and right choices if your assignment is to be successful. The seven deadly sins you toy with are not yet very powerful. But they could become so if indulged. The future will tell."

Justice eyed Skye carefully. She was there as judge and jury if Skye refused to learn from her actions.

"In this moment, there is only the present," Justice said. "My gift to you is forgiveness."

"Forgiveness!" Skye trembled with self-righteous rage. "That monster killed my friend—and for no reason. Surely you can agree what I did was fair and just."

Prudence cocked an eyebrow and Fortitude folded her arms while Hope seemed to shrink. Justice studied the young faery a moment, equanimity clear on her face.

"Let us discuss fairness," was Justice's stern reply.

The clouds suddenly parted, and the moon and stars shone. Queen Elbereth and Sister Phaena leaned in. They did not want to miss a moment.

The elusive missing kumari, Princess Devi, stilled all the winds so even in absentia she could hear this exchange. Her sweet grasses remained traumatized by the dead ogre's blood and had filed a full report with the kumari. The ageless kumari had been discreetly observing the trinity ever since.

The Seelie queen listened intently through the crystal grids of the Earth. Queen Boudica was glued to her silent crystal ball while Queen Celestia hovered nearby.

All of Olympus was also watching the events unfold. From the doomed Kingdom of Mythoses, the ancient Priestess Elanhandra was urging Elandra to wake up and be helpful. Elanhandra's husband Elthaneos's face clearly showed his deep concern. The couple had been watching over the prophecy for many eons. They knew Aurora was the one, but she needed Elandra's help. Time is a wheel, but also endless in its possibilities. All possibilities are potentials.

Elandhandra sent her message on the gentle breeze, to tickle into Elandra's ears. "All potentials may be probabilities. Yet, if one does not act with great heart and greater faith, all probabilities can fail and end up illusionary. Such are the laws of free will choice."

Elandra began to stir uneasily.

"Yes, let us discuss fairness." Skye was haughty in her tone. Vanity, the preening feminine deadly sin, laughed faintly from a safe distance away. Aurora was uneasy.

A sleepy-eyed Elandra wandered in. She became instantly alert as she looked around.

Justice was talking. "You, Skye of the Seelie kingdom and mortal Earth, have decided a life for a life is fair. An eye for an eye, so to speak."

Elandra was now as wide-eyed as anybody present.

"Yes, and it still was not enough," Skye snapped.

Several heavenly light beings recoiled, but Justice was unflappable.

"Would you wish for more in order to feed your vengeance?" inquired Justice. She sounded genuinely curious.

"Yes! I would slay him over and over every night for a hundred years if it would comfort the soul of Aethelwyn."

"Aethelwyn is well met and restored among the animal kingdom. You, faery, should know that well."

"But I miss him so," Skye blurted. Her tears at long last began to flow. "I miss him, and it hurts me."

"I see. So this is really all about you, is it not?"

Skye blinked at the harsh words. "Why, no…" she protested. Skye was confused as to how everything had gotten so twisted around.

"I dare say it is so. That, faery, is truly quite selfish of you. Do you know why the stone table had three chairs? Or why there was a stone fishing perch? Did you even wonder why there were two more mesas like the one the troll slept upon as you murdered him in his sleep without a fair fight?"

At this, the onlookers gasped. Elandra felt as if she had been slapped. *What has Skye done? Why does Aurora look as guilty as she does miserable?*

"No, Good Mother Justice, I did not stop to wonder." Skye lowered her head.

"It is because, good faery, that troll—an outcast, mixed with ogre blood, who would have brought peace between all ogres and their cousins the trolls—had a family. He fishes to provide for his wife and child. The three of them partake around the stone table in the stone chairs. The three mesas serve as their beds.

"That rounded rock formation protects their summer home. Winter is almost upon us. Mother and child went on ahead as the young one is nursing and cannot yet be separated from its mother. She is still slow and healing from her difficult childbirth. They went ahead, guided by Nyx, goddess of the night, who is not happy with you at all. The trolls and ogres are hers. She was especially delighted by this small family. I fear you have made a grave enemy."

Elandra couldn't comprehend. *Nursing mother? Child? Enemy?*

65

Skye gulped.

"Yes, good faery, you have broken all your sacred vows of balance and fealty to Mother Nature. Though they may not be learned beings, the trolls and ogres do have their ranks among the elemental kingdoms. You have disrupted all that has been worked toward. Now a young son will grow without a father to teach him hunting skills. He will never learn his father's unique diplomacy and patience.

"Moreover, that young mother will never know what fate befell the father of her child. She will not raise him in the benign ways of her husband. This mother will teach her son vengeance as a weapon against vulnerability. He will lead his people not to peace but to war against his own cousins."

Skye looked ill. Elandra thought she might retch. Aurora slipped away quietly to do just that.

"Another defeat against your virtue, good faery, is how you coerced a beloved friend to keep your darkness a festering secret, even against the one who leads your journey."

Elandra's head shot up. She sent a puzzled look to Skye, who would not meet her eyes.

"We have no secrets…" Elandra began.

Celestia whispered, "Hush!" and shook her head.

"Do you still have an appetite for more vengeance?" Justice's words were piercing. "Think carefully, good faery, for your answer shall be your fate."

The bloated and grotesque demon form of the sin Gluttony prowled the darkness, panting loudly, looking for an invitation to enter. It was salivating. It always wanted more, and vengeance was one of its favorite tools to use for the downfall of mortal beings.

Skye struggled. She did not feel bad she had evened the score, so deeply did she regret the brave Aethelwyn's death. She could see now how her poor choices might lead to another fray, but she wasn't quite ready to blame only herself. The cowardly sins stayed hidden, but she could hear them chuckling aloud in the darkness.

"Good faery," Justice continued, "how do you plea? Guilty and asking forgiveness? Not guilty, forgiving only yourself? Or is all this a mistake? Was it one simple miscommunication? Or an accident? Was your mischief intended? Explain yourself."

Skye looked deeply within. She saw how her own heart had hardened and knew she had been terribly misguided.

"Dear Justice, Mother Prudence, Hope, Fortitude, and all you others. I pray you forgive me as I learn to forgive myself and all others. This far-reaching outcome was never intended. I have deep gratitude for these new revelations, for they soften and hurt my heart. I am me again. I can see I was becoming overwhelmed by these terrible deadly sins that surround us."

Wrath, Pride with his consort Vanity, Sloth, and Gluttony all snickered. Some of them were drooling. What a coup to overcome a golden light faery!

Mother Prudence sent a sudden bolt of lightning, and the fading howls of the retreating sins brought a smile to her face. They would be back, but for now, goodness still held sway.

The mood eased. Justice spoke up in an authoritarian voice. "Little sprite and her friend, the heir descendant of Mythoses, youngsters that you still are, I applaud you. Your challenges and tests were well met. That you failed does not mean that you did not learn. This is the nature of all evolution."

Justice stood even taller. "Today, you have avoided the punishment I could have wrought. But know this: I shall be watching. I will make it my mission to keep my eye on the both of you."

Here, Justice nodded at Skye and turned her attention to Aurora, who had slunk back into the edges of the gathered group.

"Now, you," Justice turned to address Aurora directly, "do not let your blind loyalty lead you into folly. You are intended to be a queen. Not a follower."

With an incline of her head toward the other gathered holy light beings, Justice faded from sight. Mother Prudence called the other virtues aside for a counsel and pep talk that none who spied on the proceedings could hear. Occasionally, a heavenly virtue would glance over at the lone trinity of women and nod.

The three women wrapped arms around each other to stop the trembling. Thus, the trinity was reunited.

All the celestial onlookers breathed a sigh of relief, happy to know the sojourn would continue. Everyone was happy, except for one.

****

The Unseelie king growled in frustration. His chance to dominate the good faery Skye had eluded him. He was so distraught by the failure of his deadly Sins in the face of the Virtues that he would not eat or drink.

Indeed, it is written he stayed for weeks within his dark chamber, maliciously plotting his future revenge.

THE NYMPHETS

Elandra led the caravan. She was still in no mood to talk to her companions. She was greatly upset by the close call at the tribunal they had just faced.

The whole group felt dejected.

"Let us stop at this well and idle a while, oh fearless leader!" Aurora was only half-mocking. Skye sent her a frown.

"Sure. Terrific! Let's delay some more. The world might come to an end, but you would fail to notice." Elandra was not trying to hide her pique.

"Meow," Aurora sneered.

Elandra and Aurora glared at each other and then began to laugh. It was impossible for these good friends to stay angry for too long.

Skye fluttered over to the well and drew a bucket full of cold, clear water.

"Hello!" A tiny head popped up from across the well.

Skye was so surprised that she nearly dropped her full bucket. Then a second identical head popped up next to the first. Skye was flustered as the two heads turned to each other and laughed in unison.

It was only after the small heads, attached to wee but voluptuous bodies, stepped away from the well that Skye realized she was in the presence of water nymphs.

Nymphs were often described as sirens, seductresses, even succubus. They were middle-beings, somewhere between and betwixt the realms of gods and goddesses and humans. They were well respected by both. Sensual and seductive, they lived within secluded grottos, in valleys, and in watery, even boggy realms.

Nymphs would act as messengers, but they did enjoy playing both sides. While the nymphs were mischievous, they were not inherently evil or dangerous.

These two nymphets were very well endowed. Curvy from head to...*fins?* Yes, Skye thought they stood on webbed feet of sorts. The two nymphs could not stop fondling one another or themselves.

The stroking of tiny hands over full breasts and luscious hips began to mesmerize Skye. Nymphs, short for *nymphomaniacs*, were fertile and wild. Gender preferences were not an issue. The two sensual beings eyed Skye. To them she appeared bright, innocent and...delicious.

"What new hell is this?" Elandra, grumbling, reined up beside Skye. She prodded her faery friend indelicately with her foot.

Skye shook her head and came back into herself. The two small enticing beings blinked.

"What are your names?" Elandra demanded, but not unkindly. The petite women had not caused any great harm. Not yet.

The two smiled, stroking breasts and bellies, but remained silent.

Elandra swallowed and then found her voice. "We will share this water, if you will. If not, we shall fight for it."

As Elandra drew her sword, the tiny twosome gasped. The one on the left looked like she might faint from excitement. The one on the right took in Elandra's fierce countenance and slowly licked her lips.

"Elandra! What is it?" Aurora rode up, bristling and ready to spring. At the big cat energy, both nymphets looked alarmed.

"Elandra? You be her?" The nymph had a shockingly low and pleasant voice for a wee woman-fish.

The trinity of warriors felt a sexual pull pulse through them. It was not an unpleasant sensation.

"Aye. And who might you two be?" Elandra sounded fierce, but her eyes looked a little glazed.

The nymphs exchanged a knowing look and sighed.

"I am Balance," said the first.

"I am Harmony," sang out the second. "We have been sent by our mother, Bec, who guards all the sacred Wells of Wisdom. None may drink but the sages and the warriors. Our mother sends her greetings."

The two sidled closer. Harmony slid a small hand up Elandra's long leg, from ankle to knee and up, to fully massage her inner thigh. Then Harmony reached further. Elandra's head dropped back, and her mouth, along with her body, opened at the touch. She was craving to feel more, as her kundalini, magickally inspired, whispered up from her groin past her heart and head and gently exploded out of the crown at the top of her head.

Balance had hypnotized Skye, who had fluttered to the ground and pressed her lips to the wee lips of the nymph. She toyed with the clasp of her cloak and eased nude upon the ground. Faeries were also very sensual creatures, and Skye and Balance were enthralled with one another.

Aurora, who had the rutting heat of the seasonal cycles of a lioness, was immune to the nymphs. She growled deep in her throat.

Slowly the other four awoke as if from a dream. Elandra quickly recovered herself while Skye found it necessary to discreetly finish off her desire herself under her cloak. The others took no notice. Physical sensation was an accepted enjoyment. It was considered necessary in the human and all the other realms. There was no shame in that.

With a shudder, Skye came. The air around her was dizzy with color. It was Elandra who spoke.

"What is your purpose this day, besides our seduction?" Elandra wanted to sound angry, but the words came out more teasingly than she'd expected.

"Our mother sent us to warn you." Harmony still fondled her own breasts and genitals. Elandra had to break eye contact.

"Get to the point, you silly creatures." Aurora growled her words.

Sensing the red-headed warrior's impatience with their shenanigans, Harmony and Balance reluctantly stopped playing with themselves.

"Mother Bec wishes you to know Nyx has put a price upon your heads. She also made offerings to the ancient deity Shai."

At the mention of this name, both nymphets shuddered with orgasmic tremors. Shai was a genderless deity. This pangender being was also known as Fate. Shai was cunning at setting all the virtues against all vices. If Shai was their antagonist, the warrior trio was in deep trouble.

"Why would the Good Mother Bec wish to warn us?" Skye asked, floating languidly in the air. Aurora was fully annoyed now.

"It is because we two are students under the tutelage of the mother virtue Prudence. Mother Bec and Auntie Prudence are distantly related. It seems she still favors you, despite, shall we say, the fact that others have lost their heads over you." Balance smirked and then winked at

Skye.

Harmony boldly placed her hand on Elandra's rump. Elandra did not object.

Aurora growled her last warning.

"OK. OK." Harmony relented, instead sliding her fingers down the front of her own mostly open toga and fingering herself. Elandra's and Skye's eyes followed her movements.

Balance broke the mood with her laughter. "Oh, you two are so easy," she purred, fluttering her eyelashes at the two women. She then turned to confront Aurora.

"It is you, good kitty, which our mother wishes to warn. You are Aurora, goddess of the dawn. As such, you are a long-lost daughter from the lineages of Queen Elbereth and Mythoses and a foe to the lovely night-loving nymph Nyx.

"That is why Nyx is so eager to stop you. If the dawn never *comes*..." Balance looked pointedly at Aurora's crotch.

Aurora sat, legs wide open, astride her horse, wearing the men's trousers she favored. She drew her cloak over and around her body protectively. Aurora felt violated by this sensual little creature.

"Yes, if you, Aurora of the dawn, never *comes*," Harmony giggled again at the double entendre, "then the darkness wins! Nyx will reign and your trinity will be destroyed."

Harmony, motioning faster, brought herself to climax. The tip of her tongue was protruding delicately from between her lips as she let go to the spasming pleasures of her body. This time, all three women, even Aurora, looked on in envy.

Everyone was quiet for several long moments.

Finally, Skye drew in a long breath and flicked her wings. Balance started to speak, which drew their attention away from the still-squirming Harmony.

"You, cat woman, must travel to the royal court of the sun god. There, you must beg his priestess Chasca, who is kin to both you and Nyx, to side with you. Only after you win her faith, will you be able to stop the forces Shai has sent against you. Mark our words, for they are the solemn truth." Balance ruined the dramatic moment by slowly licking her lips.

Harmony gave a final spastic shudder and licked her fingers. Skye and Elandra looked away, but Aurora had begun to look as if she would like to eat the two delicious-looking nymphs. Her eyes were very bright. Too bright.

Elandra fought to distract her. "Where will we find this Temple of the Sun?" she asked.

"Simple. Just keep on until you get to the edge of the world, of course. Now you know the way to your true destiny. Too bad it waits at the edge of the world, for if you should tumble over, there will be no saving you."

With that, the two nymphomaniacs joined hands. Giving the three a parting wink, they leapt into the well.

Aurora leaped to peer down inside the wet chasm. The two vixens were gone, although none of the trinity had heard any splashes of water.

NYX OF THE NIGHT

For the very first time they finally had a destination for their quest. Too bad they had to go to the edge of the world to get there. Elandra could only hope they wouldn't trip over that edge should they ever find it.

She had heard rumors about the edge of the world. Many said it did not exist. Others said there was little chance of return should you choose to find it. It was whispered that if one fell over the edge, they would be lost in the abyss forever.

Queen Celestia was nonplussed by all of this.

"Brave Elandra, we go to find reinforcements for our purpose. It is not a hardship, but it is a necessity. Our way shall be lit through the days and nights by all the holy light beings who wish our success. It is nearly done already, little one."

Elandra held her tongue. Celestia often talked in terms of "we" and "us," but Elandra was used to going it alone. She hadn't asked for heavenly guidance. She did have to admit that as a guide, Queen Celestia had proven herself to be quite handy. For that, she was grateful.

Thus it was that the threesome set out straight west. Only Elandra knew that Celestia had once again set their course.

Very little befell the small group in the next days and weeks as they traveled. Elandra became quite tanned by the sun while the red-haired Aurora freckled. Skye soaked in the sun's rays and glowed brighter. The three warriors felt relaxed and happy. This was the way to go questing!

Queen Boudica peered through the crystal ball each

day, trying not to become impatient. She knew the temple her trinity sought was afar and that time was not truly an issue. Outcome was the key. Still, Boudica wished the warriors would hurry.

****

On the eve of the full moon, the three friends pitched camp, laughing and joking. They had not met up with any others. Food and water were plentiful. The temperatures had moderated. All seemed quiet.

It was as Elandra stepped off into the brush to shake out her blanket that she saw the beautiful stranger watching her.

"Halt! Who is it?" Elandra called out to the pale woman, who stood motionless among the evening shadows. A breeze began to blow, further obscuring the curvy woman behind her long dark hair and wispy headdress.

"I am Nyx." The words were cold. Elandra froze.

Nyx? Goddess of the night? Nyx was rumored to be visible only in glimpses. She was also rumored to be very beautiful as well as powerful. Nyx, ruler of night, could bring much fear to the unsuspecting.

"You have no business here." Elandra sounded braver than she felt.

Nyx's silvery laughter echoed out across the open spaces. "Dear mortal, you have no idea what my business—or my pleasures—are."

The sudden wind chilled Elandra. She swung her blanket around her shoulders as much for a sense of safety as for warmth.

"You shall come to a settlement of beings before you can reach the sun god's temple. Tarry there. Stay put. If

76

you abandon this doomed quest, I shall call back my assassins. If you do not heed this warning, I promise you, Fate has told me, you shall die."

Now Elandra was angry. "We'll just see about that, won't we?"

Skye and Aurora arrived, their torches of light from the fire held high and shining their way. Although Aurora had better-than-average night vision, she only saw clearly in the dark when in cat form. It was the sound of Nyx's laughter that had carried to them and alerted them. What they heard did not sound like a threat, so Aurora had not morphed. She had, however, come armed and ready just in case. They both had. Queen Celestia drifted behind them, bringing up the rear.

Nyx laughed again. A cloud obscured the moon for mere moments. When all was clear, Nyx had vanished.

****

"I tell you, she is simply trying to frighten us." Elandra stamped her foot in defiance.

"This is my fault. I have brought all of this down upon us. In my blind rage, I failed to see how harmful and far-reaching my actions could be." Skye was truly contrite.

"A lot of good that will do us now."

Skye and Elandra looked at Aurora, surprised by her gruffness. Aurora calmly gazed back. She always said what she meant.

"However we got ourselves into this," Elandra said, "let us think forward—like how to get out of it. I do not like being spied upon in the night." She was still steamed that Nyx had caught her unaware.

Patience and Perseverance chose this moment to appear. "Dear ones, continue to the temple. The nymphs have told you true."

"Great," Elandra muttered. Nyx was not the only one who had prophesized her death on this journey. Staying put in a new village had its appeal.

Fortitude strode into their circle. "Girls. Girls! All of you." Fortitude clapped her hands. "To bed. All will be better in the daylight. I can promise you that. As for your journey, I shall be with you until the end. Our odds are quite good, don't you think?"

In a wink, Fortitude was tucking the warriors into their bedrolls like children. She then set herself upon a nearby branch to watch guard over the sleeping trio.

Queen Celestia nodded in approval and left to report in to God.

ELANDRA THE PROPHET

The trio broke camp and rode out in silence. Each was immersed in her own thoughts and doubts. The world was a stranger place than they had ever imagined.

As they continued westward, the days grew longer. To the north would be the harsh desert landscape. But ahead, they were beginning to see signs of lush, tropical lands. Scented flowers were in bloom. All the flora devas giggled and gossiped as the warriors traveled by.

Skye was reminded of her assignment. Somehow, she must help the kumari become queen. Only then could Mother Earth once again reign with eternal love. What Skye did not know was that in essence, Earth would be restored to the Eden she had always been intended to be. Love would tame all beasts, even the human ones.

Skye felt restless thinking about their quest and wondering if they were any closer to accomplishing their mission.

Aurora was settling into reality. This had started as an adventure, even a lark. But she was realizing her life would never be the same should they succeed. She would become a queen! She did not doubt her ability to rule. She did fear upsetting the balances in her relationships with her friends. That made her uneasy. What would she do if Skye and Elandra moved off to another adventure without her?

By Elandra's calculations, they had been challenged by ogres, nymphets, queen of the night, the Unseelie king, and their own personal dramas. *So where is God in all this?* Celestia had not appeared in several days or nights. Elandra was feeling abandoned—*again*. She was peeved.

This seemed to be a primary theme in her life. One she felt she could do without, thank you very much.

The women agreed to ride all day. Skye was now perched backward on the rump of Elandra's horse. She was watching the grasses and flowers, which had moved aside to open up their trail and then moved back to conceal their passage. Skye waved to the flora sprites, content in her heart.

At long last, exhausted by the rhythmic motion of travel, the women pitched camp. Mother Nature had provided a floral grotto in which to sleep and dream. Fragrances sweet enough to make one's head spin and heart open surrounded them. The earth was moist. It was easy to feel the fertile life within the ground. The trinity knew they were welcomed as they sat around their small fire. Pretty sea shells littered the ground. Elandra knew shells had magic, like protective qualities, but she was thinking about the vastness of the oceans that produced them. *Who else but God could have moved an ocean?*

Skye fashioned a melodious flute from the tubular branch of a tree. The sweet notes floated in the air. The other two felt lulled.

A groggy Aurora dragged herself up. She wanted to move and leap. Keeping fit in both forms required discipline. A good attribute for a queen, she hoped. Aurora sprang out of the firelight and into the dark. Her eyes adjusted. Her nose could scent no problems on the breeze. As playful as a kitten, she bounded off.

Drowsy and content Elandra, wrapped in her cloak, dozed off. In the glow of the fire, she looked like her angelic self. She slept softly, childlike, in absolute peace. Skye knew this was a rare moment. Elandra seldom let her guard down. It made her a great warrior but sometimes an exasperating friend. Skye continued to play her music.

****

Elandra found herself wandering in darkness. There was no sense of danger, only confusion. Which way should she go to find some light?

She heard her name whispered and turned around. On the horizon was a gentle glow. As she moved toward the light, it seemed to split into two. Elandra heard amused laughing.

Celestia floated forward to her. Next to the divine one was another glowing being. Elandra stood rooted, staring.

This new celestial woman was as beautiful as Queen Celestia, although in different ways that Elandra couldn't quite put her finger on. Not knowing what else to do, Elandra curtsied.

"Rise, cherished daughter of God. Arise." Celestia sounded very formal, and Elandra wondered if she might be in some sort of trouble.

"No, dear one, no trouble. At least, no trouble yet. It is trouble I hope to avoid."

Elandra swallowed but wisely kept quiet.

"This"—Celestia turned to her radiant companion—"is Eithne. She is the queen of splendor. She rules the rainbows and colors the sunsets. Queen Eithne's miracles can be felt in every bit of nature."

"Ah, my lady, you are too kind." Eithne bowed to Celestia and then turned her brilliant smile upon Elandra. "Do you not love our queen?" she said conspiratorially.

Elandra was confused, and the dumbfounded look on her face said so.

Both sacred feminine light beings burst into delighted

laughter.

"Have you not told her, my queen?" queried Eithne.

"No, dearest, I have not. Elandra has been known to balk at authority." The two radiantly glowing beings seemed to find this particularly funny. Elandra resisted crossing her arms in annoyance.

"Precious Elandra, I am an angel of God. Celestia is my good queen. She is the queen of all guardian angels. I have been selected to come help her with you."

Queens? Guardians? Angels? God!

Elandra felt huffy. She recognized her resistance to God, a being she had never met. She did not feel God had ever been there for her, and she was unsure if she believed in God. Her obvious annoyance sent the two magnificent angels into more waves of joyous laughter.

Elandra still could not see what was so funny.

"Come. Walk with me." Queen Eithne held out her jewel-bedecked hand. Elandra self-consciously placed her hand into the hand of this celestial queen. A sensation she could only describe as flitters of bright light skittered up her arms and filled her whole body. Later, Elandra would try to compare that ecstatic feeling to a moving kundalini, or orgasm, but touching the angel was so much better. Words failed her.

When Elandra's vison cleared of sparkles, Queen Celestia was gone. Only Queen Eithne remained with her. The queen could see the questions in Elandra's eyes.

"Queen Celestia reigns over all the hierarchies of angels. Even the archangels do as she bids. Metatron is her nephew. She calls Michael to protect. Raphael is her healer. Uriel is most often her counsel, and dear Gabriel brings voice. That one is always pleased to announce the coming of God to Earth."

Elandra's head reeled.

"Do you begin to understand now?" Queen Eithne asked. "The most powerful on high are gathered to assist you. But we cannot interfere with your God-given gift of free will choice. You, Elandra, need only to truly take our hands to receive. You are only one big step away from knowing God."

Elandra looked away, not wanting Queen Eithne to see her disparaging look. The queen merely laughed and shrugged.

"Oh, it will happen, little one, for it can be no other way. You will exist over and over in eternity until you find your way home into the arms of God. He awaits you."

Elandra was tantalized but still skeptical. "God turned his face from me long ago. He shunned me. I don't know why, but he did. He decided I was unlovable. Unworthy, I guess."

Elandra was annoyed at the tears that threatened. She had never felt less like a warrior and more like an abandoned child than she did right now.

"God did not abandon you, darling. He has guided you every step. You are so very special, as is everyone. Can you understand that?"

Elandra shook her head. "I've been running and hiding from God my whole life. I feel ashamed, but I don't know why."

Queen Eithne smiled her beatific smile. "You cannot run and you cannot hide from God. He has not shunned you. You, in your childhood despair, turned your back on him. It is a theme you have replayed through many lifetimes. You deserve to be birthed into a loving family, yet you defy the one lesson that would gift you that. You must turn back to the divine light and unconditional love of God."

"You are saying that God did not betray me? That I betrayed God?" Elandra was unsure whether she felt sad or mad.

"Yes, my dearest. In effect, you cursed yourself. You placed a barrier between you and the path back to the true heavenly kingdom. Hate, betrayal, worthlessness. None of those vibrations can rise into the heavens. Until you see the lies you tell yourself for what they are, Heaven is elusive. God can be found in all things. Those are the small tastes that drive us forward in our seeking, but only God can wholeheartedly welcome you back to Heaven in unconditional love."

"I cannot deny all the beauty I see," Elandra acquiesced, "and that is God in all things. But I seem to live in a windowless chamber of mirrors. I look at myself. No matter how good or kind I may try to be, I do not see in myself a person God has loved. It is a curse."

"Only the self can curse one's own soul. God would never do that. Due to the nature of each unique soul, God would never permit another to curse someone else's soul—unless on some level that person gave permission or colluded with those low vibrations. Do you see? It must be done yourself. To curse oneself with a false belief that God does not see, know, and love you is quite like a pact with the devil. Celestial separation is a hell of its own making. It is the only hell there really is."

"God did not betray me? I betrayed myself and therefore betrayed God?"

"Yes, sweet one. Yes! You are of God. To lose faith,

respect, and hope in oneself and one's redemption is to diminish God. It dims your internal God-light. That light illuminates your way home. That is why all appeared to be so dark to you when you first arrived in this realm. You must pull your own folly up from deep within yourself and truly look at it."

"Can you have any idea of the torture it is to be so close to God and Heaven?" Elandra asked. "To sometimes glimpse it through my smoky mirrors and see it? I can hear it. I can almost feel it." Elandra indicated their still-clasped hands. "Yet, I cannot join in it!"

The despairing mortal in Elandra burst into tears, and she sank to her knees. She put her hands over her face and bowed her head in mourning. It was too overwhelming to look upon the divine Queen Eithne during this burst of sadness.

"Oh, sweet hell that I alone created," Elandra said between sobs. "I did it. I turned my back on God. I shunned God! All of eternity will damn me for that." She moaned.

"Dearest, arise. Reclaim yourself. Call to God and open your heart. He lives to be in everyone's heart."

"Don't you see? I am a terrible person. My family, our society, even Heaven—none has wanted me. What is my purpose going forward?"

"Elandra, you are a prophet. You are co-creating this world with God, as God intends it to be. All prophets are shunned by humanity, for a prophet will not collude with greed. Certainly those who feel they are above God would not be open to your messages. They are the ones who assign degradation to others. They do not wish to experience it."

Queen Eithne helped Elandra to her feet. "God cannot be shunned. He waits patiently for his children to grow up and their tantrums to be over."

Elandra closed her eyes as Queen Eithne leaned in to kiss her forehead.

When she opened her eyes, dawn had come. Elandra was still wrapped in her cloak, sleeping next to the dying fire.

Skye was packed and ready. She could feel new blessings upon the early-morning breezes.

Aurora had paced through the night. Her senses told her change was coming. She, too, was eager to be off.

CITY OF RUBICONMAS

By late afternoon on the third day, the traveling trinity could see a mirage of the village ahead.

Though the sky remained clear, a haze seemed to engulf the entire town. The three were unsure if it was fog or magic.

"What village is this anyway?" a petulant Elandra asked. She had ridden the past three days in reflective silence. Skye and Aurora had left her alone to her struggles. Sometimes quiet support was all one could offer. The virtue Fortitude was in agreement.

"It is the ancient village of Rubiconmas," the virtue Faith said, "the last stand before we reach the Temple of the Sun. One may travel this far and still change one's mind. To venture beyond the river on the other side of this fishing village, however, means no turning back. There is only going forward—through the temple."

Faith's sister, Hope, had returned to find the renewed optimism of the three friends. Hope was encouraged. She had called to Faith, who had immediately appeared to Skye and Aurora. Elandra still could not see Faith, but she felt Hope, and that buoyed her.

On the outskirts of town, small children were playing. While none were malnourished, many were very thin. They looked up hopefully as the trio approached.

"Go on with you. Scat!" Aurora flashed claws and fangs so quickly that the children could not see but could feel the big cat energy. They did not flee. Instead, they gathered closer and stopped the procession in its tracks. The smiling children blocked the trinity's way.

"Oh, alright with ye, then." Aurora broke into a smile and pulled handfuls of animal jerky from her side pack. The meat was quickly distributed, and the children gazed up at her with wonder. Aurora began to purr like a mother cat with her kittens.

A laughing Elandra scattered small gold and silver coins to the side and then quickly rapped her horse's flanks with her heels as the squealing children dove for the treasure.

As the trio passed the town's small guardians grappling for coins, Skye, still rear-facing on the rump of Elandra's horse, sent colorful showers of pixie dust over the children. Queen Eithne smiled. She had, of course, whispered the suggestion into the faery's ear. The queen of splendor was a great friend of all the Fae.

Entering town, some local dwellers, home with their chores, came out to see the procession. Small, wiry housewives shooed off the little ones with whispered instructions to bring back fathers and brothers. A rare visitation to the village was not to be missed.

A portly man approached. Bowing low, he introduced himself as the town barkeep, silver smithy, and unofficial spokesperson. Of rather small height if not girth, he obviously enjoyed a big role among the townspeople. Everyone was smiling and nodding their heads at his words.

All three warriors wrapped swords and daggers around their waists and then slid to the ground. Young boys appeared and indicated that Aurora and Elandra should hand over their horse's reins to them. Amused, they did.

The Rubiconmas Valley and waterways had been at peace for so long that weapons only existed in the ancient folklore. The trio draped their cloaks to hide the weaponry. They were not there to be threatening to the people. Their intent was quite the opposite.

Instead of being alarmed at the armor, the townspeople looked intrigued. The traveling trio felt giddy, realizing they were close to their goal of finding the sun god's temple. Everyone's mood was festive.

The entire town crowded into the public keep, filled with tables quickly laden with mugs of lager, plates of fish, and bowls of greens. Everyone had gathered to hear the tale of these travelers.

Aurora filled a large plate almost exclusively with delicious-smelling fish. Skye nibbled the fresh greens and edible flowers. Elandra had some of both but was a full mug ahead of her friends with the brew.

Belching softly, a sound that sent the nearby children into quiet fits of laughter, Elandra felt content. It was nice to be in civil society again. It was comforting to be surrounded by such peaceful, cheerful people. It felt so lovely to feel welcome.

Skye winked at Elandra, who grinned back, although perhaps a little lopsided from the ale.

****

Fiddlers arrived. Some had spoons to play upon, another had a harmonica. One laughing, red-faced man fashioned a drum of sorts from an empty beer barrel. As the music started up, couples grabbed their partners and the dancing began. Smart, concise steps allowed the swirling dancers to keep up with the wild, rousing music yet not stumble in the crowded space.

Skye took the hands of two young children and twirled them into the fray. Aurora eyed Elandra, who laughed and slid off her stool. The two friends leapt hand-in-hand to let the festive music lead their feet. For a while, their brains could be on respite.

After several dervishes, the dancing trio began to gasp for air. A number of couples had fallen out, laughing and calling for drink. Others were bundling sleepy children and heading home.

"That was fun!" Skye's eyes were vivid blue. She shone with swirling energy.

"And is it fun ye be after?" The voice was low and so quiet Skye could barely hear it.

She turned to her left and looked quizzically at the dark-haired woman who had spoken. Dressed in somber colors, her dark eyes piercing, the petite woman seemed out of place among the excited chatter.

"Hallo-o-o!" called Aurora, having caught up with Elandra in mugs of lager. "Are you hungry?"

Aurora tried to give the strange dark woman the last of her animal jerky, but she spilled off her stool instead. If the stranger had not grabbed her elbow, Aurora would be lying among the sawdust covering the floor.

"Yikes! Well, thanks." Aurora stood at a tilted angle and tried to focus on the stranger's face. She peered deeply into her new companion's eyes. "Hey, don't I know you?"

"No milady. We have not met, but we may have a lot in common. I am known as Marisha." She stuck her hand out to shake.

"Marisha, is it? I'm Aurora, this is Skye, and the unsociable one over there, looking you over suspiciously, is my good friend Elandra." Skye smiled. Elandra nodded. Marisha focused back on Aurora.

"Where are you three from, and where are you going?"

Marisha looked genuinely curious.

"We have come far, from an ancient kingdom, and are now on the final steps to finding the temple of the sun god."

"I too am traveling to the temple," Marisha said, "although mostly I have made my journey alone."

"Nonsense!" exclaimed Skye, tossing her rainbow mane of bright hair. "You must join us. We will be there in the early morning. What is your quest?"

"Ah," Marisha said, sounding indecisive and hesitant. "My mission is love." Her face fell, and she averted her eyes.

"Love, is it? Oh, how I *love* love!" The inebriated Skye clapped in delight, and sparkles lit the air around her.

"You are of the ancient Fae," Marisha said and nodded her head in respect.

Skye nodded her acknowledgment, and Elandra came closer to hear the conversation.

"You, faery, must know your magickal numbers. My name, Marisha, translates into sixty-nine." For just a second, a sexual thrill coursed through the warrior trio, although they did not understand why.

She is a temptress. Elandra's thoughts kept her wary.

Marisha turned her soulful eyes to Elandra. "No, good human. In spiritual numerology six is compassion. That is what you felt. A nine brings a spiritual journey. I bring changes. I bring endings." Her eyes pierced into Elandra's, who shuddered. "And I bring new beginnings!" Marisha fluttered her long lashes at Aurora.

"Many see me as a matchmaker. I can predict the success or failure of most relationships. Love itself is the grandest journey."

Skye and Aurora, a bit mesmerized, were nodding in agreement. Tossing her arm around the shoulder of the slender, dark woman, Aurora announced it was time to sleep. She invited Marisha to the tavern room above, the one a gold coin had rented them for the night. The room held two sets of bunking beds. Space was not an issue, but still Elandra protested.

She was immediately outweighed in opinion. Skye and Aurora turned to lead the way up the steep staircase. Marisha cast a cold, victorious smile at Elandra and turned to follow her two new friends.

Compassion, is it? Elandra grumbled. "You shall have our compassion this one night, but I shall be watching you."

Marisha flung back her head and laughed. She flicked Elandra a last glance, and Elandra swore something reptilian looked out through her eyes. In a blink, it was gone.

MARISHA'S TALE

The night passed peacefully, Elandra keeping watch for a while. All four women finally slept soundly. It was a huge relief, after months on the lonely roads, to be in a real bed under a real roof.

At dawn, a rooster crowed. The women moved and stretched, goaded by the smells of crispy rashers and potatoes. Breakfast smelled heavenly!

After eating their fill, the four women headed to the stables. There, Elandra claimed their two horses. Marisha emerged with two more. Elandra looked askance, and Marisha smiled sadly.

"I did not start my journey alone. Thus, my extra horse. I am simply grateful I do not have to finish my journey alone."

With that, Marisha handed the reins of a gentle mare over to Skye. Skye's eyes widened. The well-appointed mare was quite the offering. Without forgetting her loyal Aethelwyne, Skye recognized she was ready to love deeply again, and she reverently accepted the reins.

As the foursome trotted out of town, the children ran after them, calling out goodbyes and good wishes. The women waved.

Once away, Aurora turned to Marisha and asked about her absent companion.

"Oh, I am bitter. My heart, so easily broken, may never mend. I lost my brother. The light went out for me that awful day."

"How did he die?" Aurora was blunt and fascinated.

"He did not die. He fell to what was supposed to be his

death. But he survived. I have seen many tracings of his passage in the world. When I find him, we will join forces again. Once we are reunited, we will be whole and a family once again. The extra horse I brought for him."

"Do you think he is waiting at the temple?" Elandra was trying to discern the truth from the story.

"No, mortal. He is more likely to find us—and not in the temple of a Light god."

Again, the lizard in her eyes shone. Elandra blinked. Skye and Aurora did not seem to think this exchange was odd. She realized Marisha was capable of speaking directly into her mind. Elandra clasped Queen Boudica's nearly forgotten amulet in her hand, hidden beneath her cloak. It reassured her.

Faith whispered in Elandra's ear, "I am here, dear one. I can keep you all safe. Marisha's compassion is misguided. She has gone awry, but Heaven never gives up. I am the brilliant light of compassion. See her through me. You shall hear and see much in the temple of the sun god. Do not decide prematurely which way things must go. Sometimes our nemesis is exactly what we need to help us find God."

God again! Elandra was irritable. Marisha had rubbed her wrong, and she was unhappy to be traveling with the pushy interloper.

The goddess Faith could feel Elandra's annoyance with this intruder. Faith prodded at her. Elandra turned to the heavenly virtue, but caught herself before she glared.

"Don't poke me! Besides, what has God to do with any of this?"

Faith clapped a hand solidly on Elandra's shoulder. "Oh, ho! Moderation, little one. Remember Patience,

Harmony, Prudence, Justice, and Hope. Have not my nieces and sisters impressed upon you the need to be discerning? To witness what goes on in the world around you? I shall summon my sister Charity to help as well. Let me ask you something. If you do not believe in God, why do you so readily expect the devil to show?"

Elandra hesitated. She couldn't come up with a good response for it was fair question. Elandra felt a bit sullen and unsettled. She just didn't like the fuss her friends were making over Marisha.

Elandra's attention was suddenly diverted to a high-pitched wail that was quickly silenced. She looked around, unsure of what she had heard.

Faith, watching closely, was pleased to notice the strange shadows in Elandra's eyes clearing. Faith nodded her head sagely. She had just pried the squealing demon Envy off of Elandra's shoulder. It had dug in deep, its poisonous claws marking her skin. With a flick of heavenly light, she'd sent the disagreeable, slimy little being sailing away to be lost in the dust behind them.

SERPENT NEARS

The sun blazed so bright, the foursome of women could not stare straight ahead. Elandra focused her eyes on the back of Marisha's head, determined to see into her thoughts, but to no avail.

At midday, Celestia showed up to urge Elandra to move the party into a deeply shaded grove to rest and partake of a light supper. The others agreed gladly enough. The party halted, and the horses were turned out to graze.

Aurora bounded off in search of a simple fresh kill to roast. Skye decided to see if her cousins, the sirens of the seas, could sing some fish voluntarily into her nets that she'd cast into the brackish water. The air smelled of salt on the breeze.

Skye whispered her wishes to the nearest tree deva, which giggled and trembled before passing along Skye's message. It would soon reach the coast. If the sirens sang, Skye knew her catch would be ample for all.

Marisha was intrigued by the little faery. After Skye's fishing expedition, Marisha joined her in search of healing flowers and herbs. Skye wished to make a tea that would fortify them all, and Marisha wished to learn.

Elandra found she was gratefully alone. She fought off a yawn. She had tasked herself the night before with staying awake to watch over Marisha. Eventually, she had been lulled under by the ale she had drunk and the security of the inn. By then, Marisha and the others had been asleep for hours. All had stayed quiet. Elandra's sleep had been sweet, but short, and now she was feeling it.

As she turned, Elandra was confronted by the divine

Celestia, Queen Eithne, and the virtue Prudence. They looked at her expectantly.

"What?" *Is there nothing greater to be done than to stare at me?* Elandra was annoyed and embarrassed, although she was unsure as to why.

Queen Celestia's light laugh broke the mood. "Dear Elandra! We were just waiting for you to remember your sponsor and your duty."

Prudence winked. Eithne fluttered translucent, sparkling wings. Elandra was still perplexed. Celestia reached out and tapped Elandra over the heart where the amulet from Queen Boudica hung.

"How long do you think your good queen is going to hold her curiosity before she grows annoyed? Pull out the amulet. Call to your queen."

Elandra was chagrined. She had drawn both purpose and comfort from the amulet, but she had not realized its value as a communication device.

Hoisting it up from underneath her tunic, Elandra gazed at the now amber-colored stone. It glinted in the sun. Joy bloomed in Elandra's heart. She felt eager for news of home. She whispered Queen Boudica's name.

As she looked, Boudica's frowning face swam into view. The queen had aged. Elandra was alarmed, but the queen, spotting the road-weary Elandra, broke into her fabulous smile. All seemed well again.

"Elandra? Elandra, is that truly you? Oh, how I feared you might be hurt or lost. If you had died, I would have known, for the amulet would have blackened and gone still. How are you, dear heart? Where have your travels taken you? How are your companions? When, oh when, can we expect you home, my daughter?"

Elandra realized Boudica was both laughing and crying. This outpouring was not like her. Elandra felt loved, hugged, and chastised all at once. She grew somber.

As Elandra strove to catch the queen up, Celestia, Eithne, and Prudence held her in a bubble of bright light. She could neither be seen nor overheard while in communication with Queen Boudica about their mission. Nyx had spies everywhere.

When Elandra spoke of Marisha, Queen Boudica was grave.

"Do not turn your back on that one. She is of the Fallen. Do you understand me?" The queen was frowning.

"Fallen? She said her brother fell, but she does not believe he died. Do you know more?" Elandra was eager to be informed.

"Her brother certainly did fall! It is all humanity's hell that he did not die. Marisha chose to fall. She is one of Heaven's angels who defected and left Heaven in pursuit of her brother. Her brother is Lucifer."

Elandra gasped.

"You must get to the sun temple. There you will find friends. The son of Veritas, who is a daughter of the planet Saturn, has been enchanted and awaits you there. Queen Veritas is the mother of the seven heavenly virtues as well. They were fathered by King Zeus. King Zeus wanted to protect his lineage so that his offspring of human hybrids would never forget their true holy Oneness. He wanted them to always know themselves as sons and daughters of the one true God.

"Lucifer and his cousin Nyx, who descends from Aum, the true mother of all things and God's original consort for creation, birthed forth the seven deadly sins in response to the virtues. Ravenous and parasitic, they were set loose upon the world. They have been devouring the light in mankind ever since.

"Do not trust in Marisha. She will enjoy betraying you. Her roots have become mingled with those of the limbic brains. She is no longer divine, yet there is nothing human about her, no matter how she chooses to appear. She has the base values of fighting, feeding, fornicating, and fleeing, if necessary."

"She said she was compassionate."

Boudica scoffed. "There is no compassion, for she is a cold-blooded creature of little heart. Her weapons are sex and fear. If she cannot seduce, she will terrify. Should she succeed in tracking down her brother, she will be realigned with an evil greater than she is. Your task, I am afraid, has just gotten much harder."

Trilling laughter broke the chilly silence. Celestia bade Elandra to hurry.

"I must wind up now."

Queen Boudica said, "Promise that you will reach out to me again—and soon. Wear the amulet boldly. I shall be able to see and hear as you see and hear. Then I can research and formulate plans and actions. You need only to call my name. Godspeed, my child. My heart aches for you to come home."

With that, Queen Boudica was gone.

****

Skye and Marisha, arms laden with floral goodies, giggled their way back into camp. Elandra yawned and stretched as if she was just awakening from a delicious nap. She wanted to appear as nonchalant as possible. Skye greeted her with a hug, and Elandra replied with a huge false grin. Marisha eyed her suspiciously.

"Hallooo, sleepyhead!" Skye said. "How good for you we found herbs to fuel our energy. You might need a double dosage." Skye giggled.

Elandra looked around. The three queens—Celestia, Eithne, and Prudence—had withdrawn into the shadows but were still present.

Elandra glanced over her shoulder at a sliver of bright white light. It stabilized into the shiny silvery virtue Faith. Standing next to her was the stoic Hope. Elandra realized she was now able to see these celestial virtues. She felt proud of herself and eager to know more about their wisdom and how she could channel it to her benefit.

Noticing Marisha watching her, Elandra turned back, feeling stronger and braver than she had in a good, long while—perhaps ever. She also knew the lower-vibrational Marisha was unable to see the virtues around them. Elandra grinned.

"Let me help you with your plant medicines. I will get the mortar and pestle from my saddlebag." All friendliness, Elandra turned on her heel and strode away.

Skye looked a little dumbfounded. Marisha was uneasy. The three queens smiled in unison and slowly faded away.

WHIRLING DERVISHES

"I thought the temple was close." Aurora was grumbling. Another day and a half of dusty travel had gone by. They could smell the ocean but still had seen no trace of the temple.

"Patience, Rory. Patience," Elandra said lightly.

"Look who's talking to me about patience!" Aurora answered.

Patience herself laughed out loud and clapped her hands in amusement. Mortal women were really much more comical than their regimented male counterparts. She was enjoying this assignment.

Skye piped up. "This whole journey is about you, Aurora. Maybe you need to lead us."

Marisha began to look more interested in the conversation.

"Oho!" Aurora said. "So what now? I should do a spirited jig at sunrise to tempt the sun god?"

Only Elandra was aware they were traveling in circles. "Maybe you should," she said.

Skye laughed with delight. "Let's all dance, starting in the last of the moonlight and then greet the dawn, sky clad and with joy!"

Elandra looked at her like she was loony. Dancing in the middle of night unclothed with Marisha was not Elandra's idea of a joyful experience.

Aurora, however, looked intrigued.

As if on cue, Marisha perked right up. "Yes, my sisters. Let us worship under the moon, as it is full tonight. We shall be glorious!"

Glorious? Elandra heard the bit of vanity that had sunk its teeth into Marisha's words. She glanced at Skye, but Skye was immersed in a telepathic conversation with the Seelie queen, asking for guidance.

Aurora was having mixed feelings of dread and excitement. She wanted to move forward, yet she also wanted to crawl into a cave and hibernate until the journey sorted itself out. Recognizing her growing reluctance, feeling hindered by it, Aurora announced she was game for anything.

The women made camp and slept early. In the wee hours, they were awakened by the enchanted music of the Seelie clan musicians. Groggily, Elandra looked about.

Colorful balls of floating light swirled in rhythm to the flutes and horns. Aurora was like a kitten, batting at the floating globes in the air. The orbs seemed to giggle and float away out of reach. Aurora's hand tingled when she actually touched one.

Skye clapped in delight. "My country people have arrived!" she said. "The queen has granted leave to greet the sunrise with dance."

Skye leapt up, dropping her cloak. Sky clad, she whirled into a dance. Elandra realized the dancing orbs that surrounded them were iridescent faeries.

Marisha, who had been so keen on this celebration, was nowhere to be seen.

Elandra leapt to her feet, cloak askew, boots still on. Flinging the cumbersome cloak aside, garbed only in her tunic and amulet, Elandra strode out into the moonlight. There in the small meadow she saw a naked Marisha, streaked with slashes of what looked like blood.

Around Marisha were the vixens of Nyx. Marisha was

dancing to the gods and goddesses of the dark. She was paying homage to her brother, Lucifer, and the deadly sin demons that were her nieces and nephews.

As Elandra stepped boldly into their circle, she saw the decimated remains of a rabbit, scattered and torn in a fit of frenzy. This was the blood Marisha wore.

The energy of the dark worship broke as soon as Elandra's internal holy light disturbed the sacred rim of the devil's circle. The vixens vanished with a howl. Nyx stood quietly in the shadows, a scowl on her face.

"You there, Marisha! What devilry are you about?" Elandra was incensed.

Marisha was still writhing like a snake. She turned slitted eyes toward Elandra and hissed.

Around them, the wind stopped. Then a light began to glow. Queen Elbereth of the moon and stars stepped into view. With a motion of her hand, she banished the treacherous Nyx, who screeched and then disappeared.

Queens Celestia and Eithne, Sister Phaena, and the Seelie queen appeared together and joined Queen Elbereth in forming a tight circle of celestial light around Elandra. Skye and Aurora rushed forward to see what was happening. They stood on either side of Elandra, who stood face-to-face with the perspiring Marisha.

The sacred light was further fused by the arrival of all the virtue goddesses. Prudence had brought her students, Harmony and Balance, the nymphets with the succubus energy. Elandra almost groaned out loud.

Mother Bec stepped forward, extending a hand out to her daughters in a "stay put" motion. Harmony and Balance had the good grace to look down and stay quiet. They, like Skye, were nude. Aurora wore full fur while

Elandra shivered in her tunic.

"I am the goddess of wisdom," Mother Bec said. "You did not heed me, thus your journey has been days longer. Do not fear the dance of that she-devil, for she is spiteful but weak." Mother Bec glanced with derision at Marisha, whose nipples tightened and stood erect, in either anger or excitement. Perhaps she simply felt chilled.

"Daughter of Earth and Heaven, that amulet was a gift to you, through Queen Boudica, from me. It gives us a network of communication, but I tire of waiting to be invited in. I am here now, and I say to you to call the sun through your amulet."

Feeling slightly ambushed, Elandra stood open-mouthed.

"Yes, daughters," Bec said, addressing the others, "it is indeed time to dance the celebration of light."

Following the orders of her elders, Elandra whisked her tunic off over her head and grasped the amulet. The ambient golden glow began to brighten like a sunrise.

Aurora released her pelt and stood sky clad beside Elandra and Skye.

Marisha scowled.

Queen Elbereth turned to address her. "Daughter of God."

Marisha winced at her words.

Nonplussed, Elbereth continued. "Yes, you shall forever be a daughter of God and angel of Heaven, no matter how long your fall keeps you in darkness. Your brother's power grows weaker. You should choose more wisely, my child."

Marisha glared.

Aurora had a strong urge to lick the raw blood off of

104

her skin.

"You and my nemesis Nyx have danced with the Unseelie court this night. We are not amused."

Marisha spat at the queen, who laughed out loud.

Clapping her hands, Queen Elbereth turned back to them all. "Dance, my children. Dance with abandon! Dance with all the wildness of immense joy in your hearts. Lift your assorted wings and dance the coming dawn into being."

Spritely music began to play, and the nymphets began to writhe. Against her will, so did Marisha. Skye giggled and leapt into the air with a flourish. All around, elemental and celestial orbs bobbed and weaved. Aurora began to twirl. Elandra's foot was tapping involuntarily.

Queen Elbereth eyed Elandra. "Sometimes," she said, "the only way out is through."

Elandra nodded. There under the last vestiges of the departing full moon, the small gathering of multidimensional beings began to dance in earnest.

And dance.

And dance.

Elandra felt electrified as she twirled and swayed, all inhibitions finally gone. Her worries were all forgotten for the moment.

The women danced solo and in pairs and in sync. Their bodies knew the way. Their hearts were wide open and shining while their naked bodies glistened.

The gathered ethereal royalty had tears in their eyes. It had been eons since humans had remembered the conjoined rhythms of Heaven and Earth. Even Marisha, reluctant in her mind, could not resist the remembered vibrations of Heaven that still coursed within her DNA so many, many millennium after her leap from grace.

****

The glow from Elandra's amulet seemed to subsume the dancing females. They danced like never before. They danced to welcome the sun.

As the sun began to peek over the horizon, bathing everything in gentle light, the exhausted dancers stopped to stare in wonder. Light mixed with dawn, and the sky erupted into hues of pink, orange, and purple. The women shielded their eyes, peering forward, not sure of what they were seeing.

Where earlier there had been empty space, a gleaming mystical city now seemed to rise into view with the sun. The troupe of friends finally realized they were staring at the temple of the sun god they had been seeking. There was a collective gasp.

The gathered divinities were delighted. It took the shared joy of many to convince the sun god to show his magnificence. He had been very pleased with their dance of joy.

One by one, taking the Seelie orbs and nymphets with them, the virtues and queens along with Sister Phaena faded away. Only Queen Celestia remained, her eyes on Elandra, who stood speechless.

"Let's do hurry!" cried Skye. With a buzz of her wispy wings, she darted back to camp. The others turned to follow, eager to pack and start the day. Celestia beckoned Elandra back.

"Remember discernment, little one. You will hear and learn much. Remember, it is always and only God who lights the way, and He would have you come home again soon."

Elandra nodded, not really comprehending. Queen Celestia's words sounded like a warning, but Elandra was too filled with passion to fully take heed.

The women quickly packed up camp. Even the horses were eager. They cantered in the direction of the temple, afraid if they blinked, it might vanish.

THE SUN TEMPLE

The tall golden doors were enormous. They stood many times taller than the tallest among them. Elandra wondered what visitors could be expected that would be so large. She shivered.

Aurora reverently touched her hand to the door and said, "Please God, may it open to us."

With a groan, the doors swung inward. Aurora jumped back in surprise, but the others crowded her forward. Silently, they crept into a large but welcoming first chamber. A bright fire was blazing in a huge hearth. On a table, fragrant tea was steeping in a pot and fresh honey-topped warm bread sat nestled in a basket. Colorful fruits awaited them in silver bowls. Skye thought the food would taste like light.

"Hello, dear children. I have been waiting for you." The low trill of a woman's voice caused them to spin around. Their mouths dropped open.

There, standing radiant and dressed in golden light, stood a sparkling feminine form so bright, they could not discern her features.

"Tone it down, will you?" Marisha snapped.

The elegant figure laughed heartedly and morphed into a golden woman—beautiful, youthful, and seven feet tall. She towered over the foursome.

"Hello, Marisha. My, it has been quite a while, has it not? Lovely to see you, even though you commit to a doomed quest." The divine figure then turned to Aurora.

"Greetings to you, Princess Aurora. I am so glad Marisha has not fouled your quest in this lifetime, as she has before."

Crestfallen, Aurora looked at Marisha. "I knew you looked familiar."

Marisha shrugged, never taking her eyes from the golden woman before them.

"Welcome, other brave friends and warriors. Our temple shall serve as your home for as long as you need." The woman inclined her head to Elandra and Skye, who both dipped into pretty curtsies.

"Daughter Aurora, do you know your name means goddess of the dawn? You are the long-lost one from the lineage of Queen Elbereth, from whom the king of Mythoses drew his lineage. I am her sister. So I am also your Aunt Chasca, many times removed. My side has been easy to choose in this battle."

The other three women all turned to stare at Aurora in amazement. Marisha wet her lips like a hungry predator.

"Enter further, daughters of the kingdom. Come warm yourselves. Gather your tea and refreshments and follow me forth."

A door opened behind Chasca. The four women glimpsed a room made cozy by pillows, settees, and gently lit braziers. The air smelled like sunshine felt. There was no other way to describe it. The women, even Marisha, were swaying on their feet, feeling a bit enchanted.

They gathered up a snack and drink, for who knew how long it might be until another meal, and followed the elegant Chasca into the inner chamber. Only Elandra winced as she heard the thud of the heavy door swing shut behind them. They were sealed into a windowless room.

Sometimes the only way out is through. Elandra remembered Queen Elbereth's advice. They would simply forge ahead. She settled herself on a divan and discreetly checked for the razor-sharp knife she kept in her boot. Elandra was ready for almost anything to happen.

What she was not prepared for was the long, historical stories she was about to hear.

"My dear women, I was once a princess. I would have been queen of the twilight, where magick abounds. But I forsook that title to serve my beloved sun god. I am the priestess of this temple.

"You see, Queen Veritas, the mother of all virtues, coupled with King Zeus, then birthed the seven heavenly daughters, known as the virtues. This you already know. What you do not know is that Veritas is my grand auntie. She is also the goddess of truth, thus the natural mother of all virtue. She comes from the planet Saturn.

"I am sister to Queen Elbereth, and I was birthed on Venus. I am the protectress of young maidens. Going forward, dear Aurora, I shall be your guide, the same way the Seelie queen guides Skye and Queen Celestia guides Elandra."

Marisha's face reddened at these words. The priestess looked directly at her, smiled, and stayed silent. Marisha was fuming.

"You, Aurora, have travelled far and by faith. You are here to meet my great uncle, Prince Mahaveritas. His name means 'brave' or 'courageous,' and so he is. The prince was born of a mortal father, one who captured my aunt's heart with his kindness, good looks, and gentle manner. But never underestimate the power of the peaceful. My uncle is not to be taken lightly."

The priestess Chasca stared at Marisha. They all understood her words were directed at the outsider who had weaseled her way into their trinity. Elandra was almost excited to see what would happen next. Marisha looked deadly, like a snake about to strike.

Chasca looked nonplussed. She settled in comfortably and smiled at each visitor, one by one. Elandra reclined deeper, a bit drowsy with comfort but eager to hear more. It appeared Skye and Aurora felt the same. Marisha sat stony and silent.

"Do you know the story of all creation?"

Chasca asked this casually as if discussing the weather or asking opinions on her new dress. Elandra was sure her eyes were now bugged out she was staring so hard. After falling into a sense of lassitude after their long journey, the room of companions was now at rapt attention. Skye seemed to shiver with electrical currents, and Aurora quivered like a lioness scenting on the trail.

"In the beginning, there was the primordial mother, the fertile Aum. She was pure consciousness, filled with all possibilities but living in absolute silence. Aum was the lover and vessel to God, who desired to create, to experience the all, and be known as the Source energy of every potential.

"Aum was the seduction, and God was the knowledge. Together, they merged the masculine and feminine. They complemented each other, God's light to Aum's dark. The friction of this union created sound. Aum began to hum. She sang her own name.

"Fully merged with God, Aum began to moan and rock. In her movements was the energy of birthing. What burst forth was Oneness, or fusion. Aum, primordial mother of silence, had found her voice in her coupling with God. She sang, and the Word was born. They named

111

the Word Oneness, and God was pleased.

"To prove his vast love, God continued to create. His creations were intended to please Aum, who sang louder and longer the more she fused with God. Aum sang her ecstasy and God wanted more.

"Aum and God merged together yet again, a fusion of atoms and explosions of light and sound. Vibratory waves rocked with their passion, and thus was the Big Bang. From that ultimate climax, seas of the kundalini love energy were scattered, gifted into every being of God's mortal creations. Humanity became their favored children, and all was well.

"God, proud father that he was, asked Aum if he could grant mankind the ultimate gift. Aum nodded, pleased that her mate was so pleased. So all mankind received the immutable gift of free will choice, such was God's faith in their creations.

"God and Aum could not bear to be apart. They came together again and again. In her passion, Aum would scream out the Word and it would echo throughout time and space. All beings were born hearing the Word, or breath, of God.

"Aum went on to birth the goddesses and gods of old. She is ancestress to the Kings Zeus and Neptune. She is the mother of Saturn and Venus and also Veritas. That is why King Zeus and Veritas coupled to produce the heavenly virtues. King Zeus was safeguarding his heritage as a descendant of the true one God and Aum, his primordial mother, from any seething darkness that still remained.

"Yes, King Zeus and his sister did this, for they could foresee the battle with the fallen archangel Lucifer, who brought evil to Earth in the form of the seven demon sins. Insidiously used as weapons against mankind, the sins are deadly. A third of the total host of Heaven went with Lucifer, who pretended he wished to help and defend hapless humans against their birthright of free will choice.

"In truth, Lucifer considered humans too feckless to handle the inheritance of such power. Rather than allow humans to fend for themselves, Lucifer gifted each human with an ego. An ego was a nonstop thought process that would corrupt free will choices and disempower the masses. In their weakness, they would succumb to the seduction of that incubus dark angel. People would trade their souls for the pleasures Lucifer promised. Lucifer foretold he would become king of the planet Earth. His minions would join him, for they, too, coveted raw power."

Chasca looked directly at Marisha, whose forked tongue licked out between her lips.

"Aum," Chasca continued, "in her despair over her daughter Earth, pleaded with God to intervene. But having gifted free will choices, God could not. So Aum, primordial being that she was, coupled again with her beloved and from that desperate union, Shai was born."

Chasca paused and sipped what appeared to be pale ale from a crystal goblet. She licked her lips slowly, seductively, while staring at the unflinching Marisha. Chasca looked like a cat with a canary. The other three looked at each other, aware there were nuances they were missing.

Delicately licking the rim of her goblet, Chasca reminded the women that Shai was also known as Fate. She lived to play the virtue daughters of God against the

113

vices, or demon sins, of Lucifer.

"Shai shall gladly side with Nyx and Marisha"—
Chasca pointed to the serpentine woman—"against you as
the family of Aum. Or she might throw her lot in with all
the sacred good mothers, and their daughters, who guide
your trinity on its sacred mission." Chasca shrugged.

Marisha leapt to her feet and focused on Aurora. "Do
not listen, my pet. I have told you true. Allow me to tell
my side."

Marisha slithered more than walked over to Aurora,
where it appeared she wrapped herself around her. Elandra
blinked. Marisha appeared human again, but she was
holding Aurora folded in her arms and rocking her gently.
She had a faraway, unfocused look on her face.

Aurora felt the power of this enchantress, but the
possessive arms around her spoke to the lonely, seeking
place in her heart. She wallowed into the embrace.

Skye looked like a porcelain doll she was so still.

Marisha began to stroke Aurora, her touches beginning
to linger and become more intimate. Aurora was being
seduced, but Skye and Elandra felt they could do nothing
but watch. Watch and feel slightly envious.

"Temptress!" Chasca called. "Release that girl. She is
not intended to be one of yours."

Marisha hissed but drew back. "I am Marisha, here on
this godless planet, for my name means 'bitter one.' It is
bitter I am, you hag of a priestess. You feel so righteous
for having forsaken your throne while I am still seeking
mine. And I am so close!"

Marisha turned to the guileless women. "I am sister of
the mourning star, my brother, Lucifer. It is but one of his
many names. I have forsaken my wings and all of Heaven

to follow my brother, for I am the goddess of poor spiritual journeys, defeat, and godlessness. I am a consort and worshipper of Lucifer. I shall be seated next to him in my rightful place as queen as soon as all Heaven recognizes him as the true king of this world and all its inhabitants."

Elandra gasped. Skye looked even paler, but Aurora was gazing in adoration at Marisha. Chasca's bright laughter broke the spell.

"Foolish woman! Your brother uses you for his gain. You are but a weapon—and an expendable one, at that."

With a snap of her fingers, Chasca turned the writhing Marisha into a large dark bird. Marisha cawed in indignation.

"Silly bird. Now you have your wings back." With another snap of her fingers, the priestess engulfed the bird in wicked flames. Marisha flared, falling into ashes upon the floor. None of the other three moved a muscle.

"Come. Come now." Chasca waved to the trio, indicating they should precede her through a doorway nearly hidden in the ornately carved wall.

The three rose reluctantly. Whatever they had gotten themselves into, there appeared to be only one way out. They passed single-file through the darkened doorway. As Chasca brought up the rear, the large door slammed shut behind them. The trinity flinched at the sound.

In the now-abandoned chamber, the ashes of the defunct succubus Marisha began to swirl and float. Spinning dizzily, the ashes reformed into a figure. The body grew feathers the color of fire. It shook its head and flapped its wings.

Satisfied with its new strength, the bird rose off the ashen floor and flew upward to the ceiling. Spying an open air passage, the beautiful phoenix winged its way deeper into the temple of the sun god.

AURORA'S MISSION

"Where are you taking us?" Elandra asked.

The hallway was dim, but the flooring smooth enough that the warriors did not falter. Elandra slowed, reluctant to be in the lead, with Chasca at her back. She wasn't sure she trusted her completely.

Skye sent a sparkling cascade of lights from her fingertips. The women could see they were indeed in a corridor that appeared to have no end. Aurora, with cat eyes, could see in the dark, so she had morphed into a half-cat, half-woman figure. Although she knew Aurora could do so anytime she wished, Elandra had never actually witnessed her metamorphosis before. Still, she wasn't the least bit sure that would be the weirdest thing she would see this day.

With a small sigh, Chasca pushed to the head of the group. Raising what appeared to be a crystal wand, Chasca breathed upon the end of it and held it aloft. A merry blaze burned. Chasca turned and continued swiftly down the hallway.

The others could see the corridor was large enough to drive a wagon through. Perhaps troops had once been quartered here or barrels of wine rolled in and stored. For now, it was enough that the three friends could walk abreast of each other, drawing strength from the presence of one another.

They hurried to catch up with the priestess.

****

Arriving at an ornate, gold-leaf door, Chasca stopped. The door opened, and the trailing women could see a

117

comfortable-looking bedchamber. There were three beds and ample room for the three of them. A cheerful fire crackled in the fireplace.

Wine goblets stood ready near a large flask. Pretty feminine clothing of silks, jeweled belts, and lace mantillas hung by each bedpost. Soft, downy slippers in colors matching the gowns were tucked neatly away under each bed.

The trio was spellbound by the simple elegance of the room. It was sparsely but tastefully furnished. There were basins for washing up. Steam appeared to be rising from the depths of the three washtubs, filled to overflowing with colorful soap bubbles. Luxuriously thick towels were set out, and on each small bedside table were a brush and a comb. The lit fireplace completed the cozy feeling. Colorful flowers stood in brass containers which caught at the firelight.

"Is it adequate?" The priestess Chasca seemed anxious, as if she doubted her preparations and needed reassurance. Aurora nodded dumbly. Skye turned in a full circle and clapped her hands together, clearly delighted. Elandra was the only one who managed to stammer out words of consent.

Chasca smiled in relief.

"I am glad. We seldom house female warriors, but I heard you were coming and hoped to be properly prepared."

"Prepared for what?" Aurora's voice came out in a squeak.

"Why, to help you with your sacred quest, of course." Chasca sounded perplexed. "Do you not know why you are here?"

The three female warriors shook their heads in unison.

"Oh, dear me." Now Chasca did look a bit unsettled. "No one has explained?"

She turned to face Aurora.

"You are here, of course, to meet your true flame. The mate you cannot thrive without. The partner in your life you have longed for. Do you understand? You are here to find the one that completes you, as God completed Aum. Together, you shall restore and recreate the old kingdom of mists and myth. It has been promised that Mythoses shall rise again."

Aurora went still, thinking about her fabled twin flame.

Skye's thoughts wandered to past lovers and pleasures.

Elandra was having a visceral reaction to the mention of Mythoses.

Why does it seem I have known that place, and what does all this truly mean?

PRINCE MAHAVERITAS

Aurora awoke in the golden bedchamber, refreshed and eager. "She did say he was very handsome, didn't she?"

Skye giggled and nodded.

Elandra, unable to see how this was helping to save the ancient kingdom and find the kumari they had pledged to seek, was impatient. She rolled her eyes. "He will probably be a cantankerous old toad. He is millenniums old already."

Skye frowned at Elandra, but Aurora just laughed.

"At least he is a prince! We shall be queen and king. I think I will insist you bow before me." Aurora scooped up her satin bedsheet, wrapped it around her like a regal toga, and flounced about the room. Her nose was high up in the air, and she strove to be as haughty as she could. Even the usually serious Elandra had to laugh.

"Queen Boudica would kick your arse if she thought you were imitating her." Skye giggled.

The comment reminded Elandra of her amulet. She bade the others go on to breakfast without her. She would be along in a few minutes.

Once alone, Elandra pulled the amulet from beneath the soft dressing gown she had been provided. They had all been wonderfully provided for. Marisha seemed to have been forgotten.

The amulet shone pure gold today. Elandra peered into it, and called out softly. In moments, Queen Boudica's wavering face appeared. The concern that knit her brow cleared, and she smiled with pleasure to see Elandra looking so well.

They exchanged pleasantries. Then Elandra asked her question. "Is this Prince Mahaveritas an asset or a distraction to our sacred mission?"

Boudica laughed with delight. "Elandra, true love is always both an asset and a distraction. Fear not. If Aurora is to rule, she will need a good consort by her side. He is a very learned and wise man. Rumors of his knowledge throughout time have credited him well. It may be he will aid or advise you on your quest."

Elandra felt better. She replied she hoped they would be leaving the sun temple in a day or two to continue to search for the kumari and whatever else Aurora might require to claim her throne. The two women blew kisses, and the vision of Boudica winked out.

Elandra followed the happy voices of her friends down the long hallway and into a sunlit chamber. There, Skye and Rory were dining with a gorgeous bronze-colored man. Sunlight streaked through his brown hair, creating gold highlights. He turned his amber-colored eyes to Elandra and gave a smile that electrified her.

This unknown but magnificent god stood, bowing at Elandra's approach. Aurora giggled. Stars filled her eyes and wonder shone in her heart as she turned toward Elandra and sighed. "Isn't he dreamy?"

Everyone laughed, and the handsome man sent a warmly indulgent look toward Aurora. Sparks seemed to sizzle in the air.

Elandra went to seat herself, but their host managed to get there first, pulling out her chair and bowing low.

"Mi'lady."

His voice was like melted butter. Elandra felt warm and tingly. If this was Aurora's prince, she wondered if he had any brothers.

"Sit. Sit!" Skye was bouncing in her seat, unable to contain herself.

"This is Prince Mahaveritas! Your grace, she is Elandra, warrior and leader of our trio."

Elandra nodded, wishing just for once someone would look at her as a woman and not a warrior. After all, she had curves in all the right places, too.

The prince's eyes gleamed for a moment. Whether they had caught a ray of sunshine or he could read her thoughts, Elandra was unsure. She blushed.

Now that everyone was seated, Aurora leaned in next to the prince, slipped her arm through his, and purred. Elandra had to admit, they made a charismatic couple.

"Mahaveritas was telling us more about himself. Elandra, you need to hear this!" Skye was now clapping her hands in addition to bouncing in her chair.

Elandra had begun to peel a fragrant orange from an enormous platter of fruit. She glanced up, took in the three faces eyeing her, and with a nod, indicated the prince should continue talking.

"As I was saying, I have known throughout time that my heart would know the one I sought when I found her. I laid eyes on our beautiful Aurora, as ethereal and stunning as the Aurora Borealis I have witnessed in God's deep skies, and I just knew. I knew my long search was over."

The prince leaned in and lightly kissed the tip of Aurora's nose. Elandra stopped peeling her fruit. *Our beautiful Aurora?* Elandra felt a deep pang of loss she could not explain. She focused back in on the conversation at the mention of a coveted name.

"Yes," the prince said, "Princess Devi has been an

acolyte here at the temple for many moons. The sun god feeds her vibrant body with his rays while I feed her mind as her tutor. You see, I left my own kingdom of grace at age thirty to become a monk. Through that training, I became a tirhankara. As you know, that is a human, or human-hybrid, which through meditation and self-knowledge attains enlightenment. I could have ascended, as the masters before me, but I chose to stay and serve as a prophet of nonviolence.

"When the kumari, fleeing darkness, alighted on our doorstep, she was, of course, made welcome. Her presence here has given me purpose. I have trained her in the ancient religious ways of Yada. Its core principals are to know, to love, and to be. These are the messages of peace and harmony Princess Devi will now be able to gift to the Earth Mother and all her children. No exceptions."

"But I thought the tirhankara were just a fable!" Elandra could not stop her outburst.

"No, good sister, we are quite real. There are only a small handful of us at any given time. So far, we have hidden behind secluded walls, uninterrupted in our meditative visions. Although lately, I have begun to wonder if we are of any use, hiding away instead of wandering among the world, like prophets have been foreseen to do."

Elandra remembered being referred to as a "prophet." Queen Boudica had been her mentor, but they had rarely spoken of the elements of enlightenment this man seemed to take for granted. Now she understood how Princess Devi could be in line to be queen of love during a time of peace on Earth.

Ruefully, Elandra realized she was putting herself, and

all other warriors, out of a vocation by finding the kumari. Life could be funny that way, but peace on Earth was too tantalizing to resist.

"So, what happened next?" Elandra was trying to ignore Aurora nuzzling the prince. He did smell like sunshine and sunbaked beaches. Elandra suddenly wanted to dip in the nearby ocean.

Or maybe I just need a cold shower.

The sexually charged energy between the tawny prince and the half-cat woman was palatable.

Somehow, despite the sensual charge that warmed the air, all were able to consume a delicious breakfast and tolerate the passionate couple. Then Skye and Elandra quickly excused themselves. They slipped into the brilliantly colored courtyard. Skye was still giggling with glee.

"I think our dear Rory is in heat," she said.

Elandra nodded. "You could sizzle eggs and rashers in the air around them." This had Skye laughing out loud.

As the two wandered the brightly blooming gardens of the sun temple, Elandra began to set a return plan in motion. If they had the kumari needed for world peace, plus the prince, who was an obvious need for Aurora and would complete her ascension to the throne, there seemed to be no glitches. The prophecy to restore the Kingdom of Mythoses could come true. All they needed was to return home.

A circular rainbow of color floated down and past them. Puzzled, the two women looked at each other and then trailed the glowing orb.

They entered a different doorway into a more ornate part of the temple. Their boots tapped along the tiled floors, but if the orb could hear them following, it did not seem to mind.

Making a few twists and turns, the orb hovered near a closed double door. Skye and Elandra heard low voices and laughter from the other side. Elandra put her ear to the door, but could not distinguish the low murmurings. The orb passed effortlessly through the barrier. The perplexed duo, left behind, waited, unsure whether to knock or flee.

The door blew open inward, as if a gust of wind had pushed it, although nothing disturbed the air. Skye and Elandra were confronted by an unexpected scene.

The chamber was obviously the bedroom of Prince Mahaveritas. Gold brocade draped the windows and enormous bed. The other furnishings were understated yet elegant. This was a chamber for royalty and masculine in its richness.

Rolling to a stop on the four-poster bed were the partially clothed couple. Heat had Aurora's cheeks flushed, and her eyes were glazed. Her lips curled at the intrusion and Elandra thought she might snarl at them. The prince adjusted himself languidly, looking completely at ease.

This must be the world's fastest seduction. Elandra cocked an eyebrow.

Skye had the temerity to look embarrassed.

The glowing orb grew bigger and brighter. It began to take the shape of a woman. In moments, a striking, glowing robed woman was standing between those at the door and those on the bed. The prince's eyes got wide, and he pulled the blanket demurely over their scantily clad bodies.

"Mistress Temperance." The prince nodded in

reverence. "To what do we owe this honor?"

Despite her name, the virtue goddess was clearly annoyed—and not there for a social visit.

"My darling nephew, many times removed, greetings. I have arrived in time, I see."

"Your timing couldn't be worse," Aurora grumped. The prince gently hushed her.

"Madam Virtue, dear Aunt, I see no quarrel here, for I take to my bed the woman I plan to marry. Surely we can be forgiven our lust."

"No, my lord. I wish it were so, but the vicious demon Lust is here to test you. Lust can overshadow good judgment. Such lust can destroy love. You and Aurora have been prophesized to be the saviors of kingdoms and propagate love and peace here on Earth. Should you not first learn to love one another? Then the lust will follow quite properly.

"But lust, driven by the incubus bloodline of your heritage and the succubus cravings of an animal in rut, such as Aurora can be, makes it only too easy for the ancient and deadly sin of lust to control your destiny. To steal what is rightfully your birthright. To destroy the quest and fail the prophecies."

Elandra saw a dark, lizardy creature with a flicking tongue, move away from the nearly naked couple and slide into deep shadows behind the headboard. It had large, puffy lips it licked incessantly with a drooling tongue. Elandra could smell its fishy scent. No wonder Aurora was in bliss.

"Did you think the battle would be won upon a moment's meeting? Even now, the dark forces of evil have set against you. Lust is present. Greed, Envy, Wrath, and all the other minions of Lucifer now seek you. What, dear prince, have I always taught you? You, who have learned the sacred Yada. You, who would claim to teach another for the virtue of the entire world."

The prince pouted, looking defeated. He did not glance at Aurora or acknowledge her two dumbfounded friends. Aurora had a quizzical expression on her face.

At least she is not enraged or ready to pounce. Still, Elandra stood tense and ready.

With a sigh, the prince said, "Yes, Aunt Temperance, I was taught by you to moderate my sensuous desires. You taught me pleasure is greater when used with self-restraint. You said purity of motive and action were the test of true love and not lustful appetites. But dearest Auntie, I see my unborn children in this woman's eyes. I feel loved in her arms. I cannot be apart from her again. I have awaited her for so many lifetimes!"

Temperance seemed to melt a few degrees. The room felt only slightly cooler.

"Yes, my favorite Maha. You are quite correct. But the royal marriage must occur first. Only after the two of you have acknowledged your rare and special love and joined the powers of true flames will the human world validate your offspring as heirs to the throne. Only after Aurora has received all the gifts Heaven wishes to bestow upon her lineage, and this union, may she, as queen to her king, become the mother to your legacy."

Chastity? We're talking about virginity? Elandra was amazed. Both Aurora and the prince moved and spoke like persons of great sexual experience. Elandra had always assumed it was the passion of animal heat that would drive Aurora, but then again, *where would Aurora have found a lion to mate with her lioness?* Elandra was paying close attention.

No experiences as a lover? That gorgeous, sexy prince? Skye mused sadly. The Fae were more casual about events of the heart and twining of bodies than humans who had so many rules and judgments.

Aurora and her tantalizing prince slipped off the other end of the bed. Aurora now looked unperturbed. Donning one of the prince's dressing gowns, she turned and curtsied to the goddess Temperance.

"You of the Good Mothers, I thank you, for I quite forgot myself and my mission. I shall not fail my people or my God."

Aurora turned to Mahaveritas. "Dearest, you have my heart for all eternity. My body longs for you, but we must wait a bit longer. It shall be our day, and our forever."

Aurora stepped around the bed and glided out of the room without as much as a glance at Skye or Elandra. Stunned, they watched her leave.

When they turned back to Temperance, the smiling Prudence had joined her. Skye and Elandra suddenly understood Aurora's patient change of heart. Prudence had brought humility. To be humbled before God and witnesses was a brilliant way to quickly cool the passions of hot sexual urges.

"Young prince," the mother of all virtues directed her attention to Mahaveritas, "you, this trinity of warriors, and the kumari shall ride tomorrow for the distant kingdom they call home, where this quest began. I warn you, there are grave dangers. You are a man of peace but also a warrior trained in defense arts. Be alert. Be ready. You, Aurora, and the kumari must make it back alive."

Skye had sunk into a deep curtsy at the unexpected presence of the two holy good mothers. So she missed the sorrowful look that Prudence cast upon Elandra.

Why wouldn't Skye and I have to make it back alive? Elandra shivered in the warm air.

THE GREAT BATTLE

The morning dawned in brilliance with hues of unknown color. The original trinity of warriors thought they would never again be blessed to witness such a gorgeous sunrise. The sunsets at the temple were extra delightful, and the three were sorely tempted to remain. But duty called.

Chasca was alert and geared up for the long journey. She was also laden with weapons, Elandra couldn't help but notice. The priestess had explained she would be journeying with them as Aurora's guide and mentor moving forward. Aurora was pleased. Sister Phaena had agreed to stay on to attend the duties in the temple until a worthy replacement for the priestess could be found.

The diminutive Phaena stood under the great archway, ready to see them off and wave goodbye. The entireties of the seven heavenly virtues were also gathered. They intended to travel with the royal caravan. Their energy was light, but their mood was solemn.

Elandra was surprised to see the nymphets, Harmony and Balance, looking uncharacteristically grim, astride two ponies. The procession was awaiting Prince Mahaveritas, who was coaxing the reluctant kumari from her safe haven and into the awaiting carriage. Four magnificent horses pulled the royal transportation, already laden with extra supplies. Aurora was entitled to ride within under the protection of the others, but she insisted upon her horse. She hated to feel useless or, worse, caged in. The elegant Chasca decided to join the kumari and ride inside.

The Princess Devi emerged from the inner sanctum with no fanfare. Only the uplifting of the grim mood of her entourage indicated a change had occurred. The kumari was obscured behind veils and a billowing skirt, but it was easy to see that in stature, she was hardly more than a child. Elandra wondered what a prepubescent eternity might be like. She decided it was probably not to her taste.

So now I protect cats and children. Elandra was eager to be off, and she couldn't help but chafe at the formality of their going.

The prince escorted the kumari up and into the carriage. A driver and footman, both Fae and not anyone Elandra had met before, stood ready and staring straight ahead. *I guess Skye must have been in touch with the Seelie queen.* Elandra felt herself relaxing.

At that thought, she dragged her still-golden amulet out from under her wrap. She let it blaze visible under the sun. She felt quite sure Queen Boudica would be watching and listening.

The virtues blazed with rainbow hues. The words the *color of glory* danced through Elandra's head. She looked over at Skye, who sparkled with happiness. It was a relief to know the joyful faery felt confident.

Temperance clapped her hands. "We virtues shall lead your souls to glory."

With that, the good mothers floated forward, followed by the three warrior women, ahead of the carriage. The prince, mounted on a stallion, and the two ponies brought up the rear.

Elandra's horse pranced forward, and she felt a thrill she'd missed sorely. *Home! We are going home.*

The day was uneventful. The weather shone pleasantly.

The breeze was gentle and appreciated by the travelers. Water holes seemed to be waiting wherever the caravan stopped.

They made camp at night. The moonlight was easy to see by. The stars shone brightly, and the virtues stood watch over the camp, as they were never in need of rest. Queen Celestia appeared and nonchalantly took a seat near the trinity. Elandra was happy to see her but wondered why she was armed with sword and shield. She caught a glimpse of a dagger tucked in Celestia's tunic girdle. Despite the perfect evening, Elandra slept uneasily.

****

At the witching hour of midnight, a foreign bird call broke the silence. The horses, spooked, were rustling. One neighed and then was silent. Elandra popped up.

Drawing her sword, she looked over to see a glowing oracle of light that was the combined energies of the virtues. The seven goddesses of virtue stood solid like a wall between their encampment and the encompassing darkness. Beyond the light, Elandra heard a horse neigh, but it was not one of their horses who called. The air felt charged with danger. Elandra nudged Aurora awake with her foot. Skye was already up and scouting in the air.

The prince appeared from the shadows.

"Shhh!" he warned, finger to his lips. He nodded to the carriage and made hand gestures. He would stow the kumari in there, ready for a quick getaway. He clearly wanted Aurora to join them, but she shook her head no. Royalty or not, Aurora would never abandon her friends.

The sounds of great fluttering caused the trio to step away from the embers of the campfire in order to see better in the dark. Aurora, with her cat eyes, saw it first.

She gasped.

A phoenix was fluttering to the ground in a blaze of reds and oranges. It cawed its ugly call. As its talons touched the earth, it transformed into a bigger, stronger version of Marisha, sister to all things evil. Elandra drew her sword.

The goddess Nyx strode out of the shadows, her beauty outshining Marisha's scowling countenance. Nyx beckoned to someone. A voice rang out.

"Nay, dearest Nyx. I do not stand for you. I also do not stand for the heavenly lighted ones. I am Shai, the divine fate. I shall be the last one standing, if need be, to determine this outcome between the holy light and dark." A form moved under the moonlight.

It was impossible to discern if Shai was inhabiting a gender. The figure was tall, regal, and shrouded in robes and a hood. Elandra's scalp prickled. Aurora rumbled a low growl. Her claws were visible, even though she held her sword and shield aloft.

The wind kicked up, and with a flash of stinging light, there stood Celestia, Chasca, Elbereth, and Eithne. Elandra began to relax. It seemed they had a whole army against Marisha and Nyx.

Marisha threw her head back and laughed. Turning coquettishly, she called over her shoulder. A shadow, darker than darkness, loomed behind her.

"Is that Lucifer himself?" Skye whispered, having landed silently behind her two friends. Elandra was unsure if she was more startled by the sudden appearance of Skye or the Prince of Darkness.

"What say you, dark prince?"

The Seelie queen materialized wrapped in faery

adornment. She looked fierce. Her shining troops appeared and gathered around her.

A deep, roiling laughter rent the air. The trinity of human hybrids felt nauseous.

A darker shadow broke from the ordinary shadows. It was the Unseelie king with his armies. The Fae warriors would be matched on either side.

Sniggering, chortling, fuming noises drew closer. The seven deadly sin demons stood in a line opposite the wall of seven divine virtues. They were matched one to one.

Harmony and Balance reluctantly moved forward, prodded by their mother, Bec. Bec would yield no sword but was wise in the planning and formations of battle. Her presence felt like a good omen.

Crashing footsteps thudded nearer. A small band of wicked-looking trolls and their cousins had arrived. They arranged themselves behind Marisha. The smaller troll in front had a baby strapped to her back and brandished pitchforks in each hand. She glared at Skye. Elandra was pretty sure she knew who this troll who wanted to skewer them was. She was suddenly feeling outnumbered.

The coach driver and footman had silently attached horses to the carriage and saddled the rest. They stood ready for orders. Elandra saw the kumari's veils fluttering through the coach windows. She had been readied to escape.

The sound of solid strides had the warrior women turning to see who joined them. Prince Mahaveritas, ablaze in golden armor, stepped up, sword ready. He had an easy, excited look, as if this was jousting for fun. His confidence inspired the others. Aurora narrowed her eyes and began to purr.

Elandra felt a momentary lick of envy for her friend's great luck in finding such a man. But the demon Envy snickered, as if reading her mind. Elandra drew her attention back to the forming battle.

Queen Celestia, not to be outdone by Lucifer, summoned four of the great archangels. They muted their fierce light, but still the battlefield lit in sharp contrast to the dark. The ogres and trolls stepped back, momentarily blinded, then snarled with rage. Marisha's laughter rang out.

Nyx sent clouds to dim the moon and starlight. Elbereth whisked them away. The Seelie queen set a faery ring of magicked fires. The Unseelie king smothered them with a flick of his wrist.

The kumari, already queen of the devas, sent a message of joy and laughter rippling through the adjoined root systems of her plants and trees. It was like an enormous energetic tickle. The plants giggled, and the dark forces roared in pain.

A vision of gossamer light appeared from the sidelines. In strode an ageless being. Celestial and regal, she tossed her flaming mane of red hair, and smiled at all the good mothers. Those on the enemy's side voiced their consternation.

"'Tis Queen Clementia!" Skye leaned in to whisper to Elandra and Aurora. "She is goddess of forgiveness, daughter to the primordial energy many will someday call Quan Yin, the goddess of compassion in embodiment. She is grandmother to all these good mothers." Skye was in awe.

"I am here," Queen Clementia proclaimed, "and I shall judge these proceedings independent of Shai. There shall

135

be two, not one, who judge you. Plus God himself, the only one who may judge us all. Be aware! All Heaven is watching." She receded to the sidelines.

A chilling, deep, guttural voice growled a laugh. "Remember, Good Grandmother, all hell hath been loosed upon Earth while your God watches."

"Be afraid, Lucifer. Be very afraid!" Queen Clementia was tormenting the fallen archangel with her words. Elandra hoped she knew what she was doing.

Drifting in softly beside the virtues, two winged goddesses landed. They were defiant and hard to look upon. Mahaveritas frowned.

"They are Valeria and Kyrie, twin angels of death," he whispered.

"They have a particular grudge with the demon Sloth," Queen Clementia announced. "Sloth bespells so many to waste away, or to take their own lives before their time, and even by their own hand. It is sinful. After a battle, the death twins take all good souls to Heaven." Queen Clementia nodded a greeting to them.

Elandra was so busy wondering about the fate of her own soul, she nearly missed the rest of the queen's words.

"These twins married human soldiers. They birthed the warrior women of legend. The Valkyries are their offspring."

Elandra's hope flourished. It was rumored she was distantly related to the Valkyries. This was as close to blood family as she had ever been. Her amulet was flashing in the light of the archangels. Elandra knew Queen Boudica must be praying for them.

A hideous screech broke the silence, and three dark shapes bulleted to the ground. When they arose, the three warrior friends and even the prince gasped.

"Queen Clementia." Marisha was mocking in her tone. "Since you brought twins, I match you with triplets. This deliciously evil trinity is Libitania, the goddess of corpses and funerals. She enjoys mutilation. Next to her is Macaria. She is the renderer of a death so slow that many shall beg her for swiftness. She delights in torture. This last one is a special friend of mine. Her name means 'misery.' I shall let her introduce herself."

A black crone, vulture-like in appearance, stepped forward. In a hollow voice that brought chills to those gathered, she said, "I am Oizys, daughter of Nyx." She turned and faced the beautiful shadow woman. "Hello, Mother."

"My dearest daughter, a pleasure to wreak carnage with you again." Nyx laughed. Oizys laughed with her, but her laugh was an odd croaking sound.

"Enough!" Lucifer bellowed. "A kingdom to the one who brings me the prince's head and the heart of the kumari. The rest are carrion fodder for the predators."

Elandra now fully grasped the significance of the prince and kumari being sheltered in a temple of light where the dark had never been able to reach them. But the dark had patiently waited for this very moment.

Light flashed. Alala, goddess of war, appeared. She took no sides but yodeled the war cry, signifying the battle to begin. She would also cry the final battle cry in victory for the winning side. In her bright presence, the dark, unable to overcome her arrival, receded. Her war cry brought them forward again.

The two groups merged into battle. Swords swung and blood sprayed. No one knew whose blood or gore they wore. As long as they could still fight, none cared.

Marisha maneuvered herself to confront Aurora. "You beast!" she hissed.

Elandra stepped in, sword raised. "You serpent," she sneered.

Marisha's eyes glowed as the reptile within her stared with hatred at Elandra. With a flick of a forked tongue, she lunged, but toward Aurora, not Elandra. Mahaveritas spun Aurora out of danger. Before he could attack, Elandra had drawn Marisha's blood. It ran black as ink. Marisha bellowed like a crazed monster.

At her cry, attention flew to the battling women. Marisha was good in the art of combat, but Elandra was better. Their razor-sharp swords flashed and stabbed. Their shields were put to great use. So mesmerized were the forces of dark—Lucifer seemed genuinely amused—that the enemy failed to notice Mahaveritas push a struggling Aurora into the carriage.

He leapt aboard, grabbing the reins and slapping them down on the straining horses. Eager to be away from battle, the horses surged the carriage forward and they were quickly out of view.

Elandra witnessed this as best she could from the corner of her eye. She was elated. Whatever the battle's outcome, the future queen and king had escaped with the world's best chance for peace on Earth. She wished the royal couple happiness and wished the tiny kumari good luck. Grimly, Elandra bore down on the fatiguing Marisha.

As the battle between holy light and dark wore on, Elandra had Marisha on the ground, blade to her throat. *It would be so easy to slit that snake's throat.*

Elandra debated. The virtue Charity materialized near

them in petite goddess form. She was frantically shaking her head no.

Marisha blinked, and her reptile eyes were gone. Her human eyes filled with sorrow.

"Go on. Do it! Run my life blood into the ground with no chance for redemption. Those angels of death will never carry me. My own brother, Lucifer, has betrayed me. I have used my own free will choice to leave Heaven and never return. Kill me! You do me a favor."

Still, Elandra hesitated. She had been trained for this. You never let a professed enemy live to come at you again. But this poor, miserable creature, all alone, betrayed by family, lost to God, and misplaced among humans touched her heart in way that surprised Elandra.

She gave Marisha a swift kick in the ribs to slow her down and then strode forward to meet the onslaught of ghouls.

One by one, the fighters fell or deserted. The holy ones, like the unholy ones, could not be killed or suffer. Elandra feared the war would be endless. Queen Celestia appeared and grabbed Elandra's gloved hand.

"Elandra, the carriage is long off and away. Fear not, for this battle is won. I will pull my legions of angels. We go to protect the royal couple and Princess Devi. The Seelie queen will draw off the Unseelie king and disperse his minions with her fiercest warriors. That evil trinity is picking through the dying like the predators they are. The angelic death twins are escorting souls to Heaven. Nyx has left, for night fades. Queen Elbereth and the others are off to see to their celestial duties.

"The seven heavenly virtues and the seven sin demons are well matched. A temporary truce has been called

139

between them. The goddess Alala will be chanting our victory and the ending of this battle. You and Skye must flee! Get to your horses and ride the road you know. You will intercept us after a day and a half's long ride. Together, we go back victorious to Queen Boudica."

Elandra looked deeply into Celestia's eyes. "Thank you, my queen, my tutor, and my guide." She bowed low over the hand she held.

Queen Celestia brushed Elandra's hair back from her face. "Child, do not let your guard down, for your lessons are not yet complete." Her words were soft and for some reason sounded sad. Elandra wondered why. When she looked up, Celestia was gone.

"Hurry, Elandra. Come now!" Skye galloped askew in the saddle of her horse, dragging the reins of Elandra's wild-eyed steed. The horse smelled all the blood.

Skye's mare had scented the handsome stallion abandoned by Prince Mahaveritas. Both mounts were skittish and hard to control.

Skye flipped the reins to Elandra, who fought to stirrup her foot on the churning horse.

"Follow me!" Skye raced for an opening in the carnage. She was moving too quickly to be stopped and she trusted Elandra was at her heels.

Elandra's foot caught, and she was hoisting herself into the saddle when strong arms snaked across her throat and shoulders. With a tug, she was knocked loose from the stirrups and pitched to the ground.

Her terrified horse galloped off without her as Marisha set a sharp blade to her throat. Elandra's own weapons were sheathed.

Always pay attention to who is coming up behind you.

140

Belatedly, Elandra was remembering this teaching from Queen Boudica. She had forgotten in practice, and now, circumstances were very real.

The goddess Alala sent a war cry of victory for the side of heavenly light, but Elandra was quite certain she would be one more casualty of war.

THE TRIBUNAL

Elandra stood still, head down. A hasty tribunal had been gathered. Lucifer, as ugly as his reputation, presided.

"The question," he said, "is not whether you will die, but whether you will beg for mercy at the hands of the triplets of torture or die swiftly by Marisha's blade as the death twins watch, unable to take your forgotten soul to Heaven." He roared with laughter.

Libitania, Marcaria, and Oizys were salivating. Valeria and Kyrie stood stoic, no emotions showing. Elandra felt oddly grateful for their presence.

The troll mother lifted up her son so he could glare at Elandra, too.

"See her? Do you see her? That is the witch who killed your father! Murder. Murderess!"

Elandra did a slow burn. She had done nothing wrong, but she could never betray Skye by telling the truth. The evil triplets looked petulant. If no one was suffering, being humiliated, degraded, or tortured, they were bored.

Queen Clementia made an appearance. "I wish to have a word with Elandra."

"No." Lucifer dismissed her with a single word.

Clementia laughed. "Of course I can talk to her. No need for you to be so polite." The queen cocked her eyebrow and Lucifer sulked.

Marisha, who had been sitting on the ground in her brother's shadow, leapt up in anger. She strode forward. "The prisoner is mine!"

Queen Clementia shooed her away with the wave of her hand. "Tiresome child. Do learn some manners. It is written in the Heavens that any who are to be tried, or are doomed, are allowed to repent. Elandra has every right to ask forgiveness of herself for her anger. God is not angry with her, so no other forgiveness is needed."

Queen Clementia turned toward Elandra. "Well, dear?"

Elandra fought not to tremble with anger more than in fear. *God again?* Elandra looked through her life. She had things she still wanted to do. Things she still dreamed. If there was a God, he was indeed still angry or he would not have led her into this trap. Surely a crisis of faith was not worth bargaining for with her life.

The pangender deity Shai stepped forward. Fatal choices must be made, and they were hers to make. She peered deeply into Elandra's eyes and felt into her breaking heart. There was so much pain there. Far too much pain. The immovable Shai was stunned and then saddened.

"God have mercy on your soul," Shai whispered.

"God has no mercy for my soul," Elandra snapped back. Her eyes widened in surprise as blood began to bubble from her mouth.

The point of Marisha's sharp sword had penetrated Elandra's body and now protruded through her heart and out from between her breasts. Marisha had pierced her from behind with no judgment, no permission, and no good reason. The triplets drooled and groaned. They wished to feast on Elandra, yet would have greatly preferred a long, drawn-out torture.

Queen Clementia caught Elandra as she fell and eased her onto the ground. Valeria and Kyrie moved in to stand guard. The future of this mortal's soul had not yet been determined.

Celestia appeared. She was full of grief but also quiet acceptance. The odds had never been good that God would win this wounded mortal over in this lifetime. She bowed her head.

****

Through the amulet, Queen Boudica watched the whole event. She cried out, but none could hear her. The spunky child, who had been like a daughter to her, had been slain on the quest to deliver the kingdom to its rightful queen and king and to prosper love and peace among humanity. Boudica could not see how a loving God could still refuse the unrepentant Elandra into Heaven.

"Because he must."

Boudica turned to see Queen Elbereth standing in her celestial glory. She smiled sadly. "Elandra did not forgive. She is dying, her face still turned from God. Such is her pain. This is her free will choice. God cannot intervene, even to save her soul. I wish it could be some other way."

Queen turned to queen and they held each other as their grief over losing Elandra finally hit home.

****

Queen Clementia held the dying half-mortal. Her eternal soul had to go somewhere. Heaven was closed to her. Surely, Lucifer and his legions of dark souls were too harsh a punishment for the half-angel who had tried to be good. Charity sobbed beside her. She was nearly beside herself.

"When I shook my head "no" at Elandra, I did not mean she should spare Marisha when she had her blade to her throat. I meant *no, do not let her live.* The world would be a better place without Marisha. Elandra never trusted in her, yet through her kindness, she spared her. Elandra was too nice. It is never charitable to one's self to give away so much to another, as Elandra did in letting Marisha live, that it causes self-harm. I fear she misunderstood this, and me. Elandra made herself too vulnerable, and now it has caused her downfall."

Queen Clementia inclined her head toward Charity. "Dear one, no. Our Elandra's heart is big enough to feel compassion toward all but her own self. You did nothing to change her fate."

The queen plastered a smile on her face, even though anyone could see the pain in her eyes. Her face was the last thing Elandra would see. Queen Clementia forced her pain away and swelled with love. Elandra's last memory would be the smiling face of someone who loved her dearly.

Gurgling noises came from Elandra's throat. She was trying to speak. Queen Clementia, not heeding the blood, leaned in closer.

"Tell...tell God...I am sorry." Elandra smiled up at Clementia. Her life force began to slowly lift from her body, and her once-lively blue eyes went blank. Her body slumped. Death had claimed her.

Queen Celestia had sent an army of angels to guard Elandra's body. The twin angels of death still stood by her side and her drifting soul. Kyrie reached out, gathered the departing light body, and wrapped Elandra's soul in a special net for transporting it. The question now was *where was Elandra's soul supposed to be delivered?*

The angels were prepared to guard this tiny, fallen being until their queen returned. Bored, the evil triplets flapped away. Lucifer had openly scolded Marisha for allowing Elandra to die so easily. Marisha had then gone off sulking.

With nothing left to see or do, camp was broken. All the gathered beings dispersed in silence. Their dark master was not happy that the prizes he coveted had escaped. Heads would roll.

The archangels still traveled with the carriage. They were alert, powerful, and ready for vengeance against evil. To be stabbed from behind during her repentance tribunal had robbed Elandra of a true warrior's death. The archangel Michael in particular was miffed.

None would try again to interfere with the swift passage of the royal carriage back to its fabled homeland.

HOMECOMING

Many leagues of distance passed swiftly. The divinely escorted carriage rolled, invisible and silent, through all the dimensions of Middle Earth. No one spoke much. They were all grieving. They had been advised a few mourning celestial beings were still left on the battlefield to help tend to Elandra and the aftermath of her sacrifice. Their carriage was *not* to turn back. It was over but not forgotten.

Aurora and Skye rode as scouts. They looked for evil but found none. They looked for God in all things, but their hearts remained heavy. Even the birds stayed silent. Skye blamed herself, although no one else did.

As dawn broke on another uneventful day, the troupe could see in the distance the watchtowers and walls of their nearing kingdom. Small, colorful flags flew at half-mast. As they drew closer, the sea-salt-scented air surrounded them. Everyone's spirits began to lift. Those who were left from the quest would soon be home again.

A fanfare of horns and celestial trumpets blared. A parade formed outside the gates. People laughed and jostled. Their salvation had arrived at last.

The small but regal procession rode humbly through the gates, once again protected by walls. The entourage stopped at the castle steps. Queen Boudica, in all her splendor, stood waiting. A smiling Corban stood by her side. The glow over the kingdom was bright enough to let all beings know that Heaven, the virtues, the Seelie, and all the other beneficent gods and goddesses of history were present. This moment had been long awaited.

Aurora and Skye dismounted. Breaking all protocol, they raced up the steps and into the loving arms of Queen Boudica. The women embraced, and the tears flowed. They could not be stopped.

Boudica gathered herself first, proclaiming in a wavering voice that victory was theirs. A roar rose among the people. Everyone was happy and excited. Queen Boudica quietly bid the two warriors to stand in their grace. There would be time to mourn Elandra later.

The carriage door was opened by Prince Mahaveritas. He handed down first the imposing Chasca, then the kumari. Within their royal presence, the crowd grew silent with awe.

Chasca, former priestess of the temple of the sun god, instructress to Prince Mahaveritas, goddess of twilight, former princess, sister to Queen Elbereth, and kin to the goddess Venus herself, strode forward and formally curtsied.

"My queen," she began. "I am Chasca, protector of young maidens. I deliver to you a virtuous Aurora, goddess of the dawn, myth to the were-people, and long-lost daughter to the lineage of Queen Elbereth, and therefore, my niece and descendant of the great mother Venus. She is intact, pure, and wise. She shall ascend to the throne, which is rightfully hers by her blood lineage. I shall remain as her aunt, guide, and teacher, as I shall also remain as tutor to the prince-who-will-be-king."

The crowd released its collective breath.

"Welcome, holy Chasca and all our otherworldly friends. You have been long awaited. Prophesy did not do your heavenly light enough justice."

Chasca rose at the kind words and turned.

148

"My queen, I present the kumari—Princess Devi, primordial divine child. She is girl, maiden, and queen of the deva kingdom. Now she soon takes her place in our world as the Queen of Love. We shall all have peace and golden times ahead."

A cheer went up.

The diminutive kumari removed her face veil. Startling large eyes looked out from an eager, young face. She lifted her hands gently up into the air.

"Mother! Father!" she called in a soft voice. "It is time to sing."

The Aum sound was heard, softly at first, growing louder and longer. It birthed vibrations into being that mankind had never remembered hearing or feeling before. That vibration was Oneness.

It was recorded that in that moment, women and men of all ages and ranks felt a tug in their sacral area. Many reported a tickling sensation that arose slowly, and delightedly, up the body and out the top of the head. Others would argue it was a zip of lightning that raced up their spine and through their crown chakras. Others just felt pleasant chills or feathery movements and wondered what was to come.

Thus it was that the kumari, having been delivered, awakened the sleeping seeds of kundalini love energy in every being of God's mortal creations. As love began to flourish, fear and hate would begin to dwindle away. As the powerful Aum potentiated, everyone stood blissfully frozen. As it began to fade, whether it was moments, weeks, or years, none could tell. Everyone was blinking, awake, and looking around wonderingly.

Queen Boudica, Skye, and Aurora, in that moment,

knew in their hearts that Elandra's sacrifice had not been in vain. Peace held the kingdom.

Aurora caught the eye of her much beloved Prince Mahaveritas and smiled. He blew her a kiss and a wink that held both love and mischief.

The whole kingdom, in celebration, began to plan the royal wedding, the likes of which had been told in the stories of long ago. The kitchens, farmers, textile weavers, attendants, and gardeners were given just ten days and nights to create the event. Aurora could hardly wait to be married to her prince!

The soon-to-be love queen Devi sent invitations across the lands by the root systems of her plant people. The Seelie queen bade her wanderers to drum the message out to all the dimensions of light beings. The nymphets resounded the invite in a siren's song that no one could resist. Skye sent the message on the wings of her butterflies. It was a happy time in the ancient kingdom.

THE VERDICT

Back at the battlefield, Queen Celestia and her guardian angels stood watch over Elandra. They allowed no scavengers or flies to draw near. Quan Yin, goddess energy of compassion, grandmother to all the good mothers, had blessed Elandra to remain intact. Decay would not mar her physical beauty any more than darkness had been able to mar her shiny soul.

Queen Clementia, daughter many times removed of Quan Yin, returned from her role as advisor to Heaven. It was with relief that the others saw she was smiling.

"Hail, good queen," greeted Queen Celestia, directing air kisses to both of Clementia's radiant cheeks. "How goes the universe within you?"

"Dear sister, the Heavens and Earth are good within me. It has been decided. Our brave child, Elandra, in her last breath, asked God's forgiveness. As she is of God, it has been decided that by default, she also asked herself for forgiveness. She cannot be banished into the darkness."

A banshee howl arose. The evil triplets, who had continued to lurk in hopes of capturing Elandra in death, soared into the netherscape. Their time here was lost and done.

Celestia smiled. "Am I to hope that our Elandra is to be admitted into Heaven after all?"

Her smile faded at the expression on Queen Clementia's face. Clouds momentarily obscured the sun.

"Not so, good queen, for it was not enough. Elandra left us one breath short of her redemption. She will need to return and replay this lesson again. Her name then will be

Jeanne d'Arc, or Joan of Arc in many history books to come. She will fight for a cowardly French king, who shall betray her. She will suffer and die at the hands of ignorant men. But she shall deliver the crown, secure her personal dignity, and die boldly, with great faith in her God.

"After that lifetime, her story will be told. The stories of all the female warriors throughout time will be acknowledged by God through his forgiveness and compassion. Valeria and Kyrie shall be the ones to go back and escort their own offspring, the Valkyries, to Heaven. They will also escort Elandra, as Joan. She will finally be reunited with her divine family again after having been the sole survivor of their human side all these many lifetimes."

Queen Celestia blinked, disappointed. "Dearest, although we are outside of time, this is not a near event. What shall be done to honor Elandra in this lifetime?"

Queen Clementia smiled broadly. Valeria and Kyrie materialized into view.

"It is an honor and privilege to the twins," Queen Clementia said, "to escort one of their own to the top of Mount Olympus. King Zeus has graciously agreed to house Elandra and give her all the time and healing she may need before beginning a new lifetime on her great spiral homeward. Her dharma wheel will move forward, aided by her past self as Elanhandra, who then comes full circle and may return to God's Heaven. Thus is the limitlessness of time as a wheel. Also present is her twin flame and mate Elthaneos. He will never desert our Elandra, in any lifetime. They shall meet again and again; lifetime after lifetime, until Elandra regains her angel wings and desires to live once again in the Heavens."

"Once again?" The death twins looked confused.

"Oh, yes. Elandra was among the fallen angels who sided with Lucifer against God over free will choice for humans. Unlike Marisha, who swore to never return and slammed and locked the door to Heaven closed in order to forever remain with her brother, the prince of darkness, Elandra left to help humanity. She didn't have a long-term plan and was not opposed to returning to Heaven someday."

Startled, Queen Celestial laughed her sparkling-clear laugh. "That certainly sounds like our impetuous Elandra."

"Yes, but this time, I will be tutoring her." The goddess virtue Justice appeared. "We shall finish her lessons in patience, nonjudgment, and forgiveness. Proper forgiveness starts with self. It is only after forgiving oneself that a mortal can truly forgive others."

Prudence appeared next to Justice. "Yes, we virtues shall be biding our time between Olympus and the new kingdom Elandra died for. When people learn to be content, in whatever circumstances they are in, the kumari's peace will be won. The seven deadly sins will cease to exist on Earth."

With beatific smiles, the two fabled virtues shimmered and disappeared.

MOUNT OLYMPUS

Elandra opened her eyes and looked around. She sat up with a start. What she had thought was her reflection in an overhead mirror was moving and speaking to her. Groggy, Elandra peered at the dazzling woman by her side.

"Why do you look like me?" she asked.

The woman's laugh was a joyful twitter. "Perhaps there is something about you that I love about myself." The woman winked.

Elandra heard male laughter and turned.

When she saw Elthaneos, she sucked in her breath. Her doppelgänger was immediately forgotten. This man was gorgeous! Tall, fit, tan, smiling, and *smokin' hot*. Elandra blew out a breath.

The woman who had awakened her took the male warrior's hand in hers.

Elandra felt crushed. He was already claimed. That much was obvious. *Perhaps he has a brother or a cousin?* Elandra fanaticized a moment before bringing her attention back to the spacious, airy, white marbled room.

"Where am I?"

"On the very top of Mount Olympus. Father Zeus and Father Time have colluded to allow you to be here both as present-day Elandra and to reside with me, Elanhandra, as a past-life Elandra. I am you. Elthaneos and I, as guardians, witnessed the original destruction of the kingdom you have fought to heal. We have guarded the prophecy. It was always our prerogative to save the Mythoses kingdom, but it was not yet our time."

"Our time?" Elandra looked askance at the handsome

154

man.

"Yes, my dearly beloved. You have been known to me since our original time in Heaven. I follow you throughout time, scenting your love and loyalty. We live again, over and over together, and ever it shall be." He winked.

A blushing Elandra glanced over to see if Elanhandra was offended, but she merely laughed.

"Being outside of time and space is not always an easy human concept, but I promise you, it works quite well." Elanhandra took Elandra's hand. The energy tingled between them. Elanhandra used her other hand to draw Elandra up and off the divan where she had been sleeping. She led her to look out a window.

There, floating far, far below the layers of clouds and rays of sunshine rotated a glowing green and blue Earth. Elandra sucked in her breath.

"Oh, my!" She breathed out.

"Yes, quite a view. We always have what you might call 'ringside seats' to all the most glorious events, even holy battles. Here, we are allowed to intrude on ourselves. It was I who whispered into your heart to ask for God's forgiveness with your last breath. You would not have used that breath to forgive yourself, but these are the human peculiarities we learn from.

"You have saved your kingdom. You have found its true queen and reunited her with her king. The kumari has been delivered, and every human heart grows in love. Tell me, dearest Elandra, is there something in your past life you would have changed? Especially knowing that to change one thing could mean a different outcome to your quest? Look into your heart. Is there anything for which you cannot forgive yourself or another? Are you still angry with God for your misfortunes?"

Elandra reached within, where all she could find was peace. She smiled into the knowing face of the other Elandra.

"You know me pretty well, don't you?"

"Of course. I am you!" Both Elandras laughed out loud.

Elthaneos smiled broadly and offered each Elandra an arm.

"My ladies." He indicated an archway with a nod of his head. Thus Elandra was blessed to give herself a tour of the legendary heavens below Heaven.

Olympus was pure light and joy. Music and fragrances swirled in the refined air. All the gods and goddesses of mythology nodded in acknowledgment of the healing, holy trio.

"Elandra, my dear little one, we shall be here until after the gifting, the wedding, and the splendor. Then it will be time for us to return into God's own Source energy, to be replenished, ascended, and readied for our next earthly assignment." She gave Elandra's arm a squeeze.

Elthaneos turned to her. "It will not be in your pivotal life as Joan of Arc that we shall meet again. But I swear this to you, on my heart and soul, we do meet again. Again and again. Twin flames, having fanned the fires, never die out."

He leaned in to kiss her hand. Elandra was electrified at his touch. Recovered from death, her human kundalini spun crazily up her spine to shoot sparks up off the top of her head. The others laughed, but she didn't care. This was a world of love. A world the likes of which Earth was aspiring to. In love there could be no shame, no guilt, no fear, and no betrayals. Just divine Oneness. Elandra knew she understood at last.

A little bird alighted on the balustrade. Elanhandra, the past-life Elandra, stepped over to it and whispered. The bird began to twitter. Elanhandra whistled a bit. The bird whistled back. She sang a melodious song, and the bird matched her perfectly. The woman and bird seemed to wink at one another. Present-day Elandra clapped her hands in glee.

"What a song of joy!"

Elthaneos explained. "It is your song, dear Elandra. Our song together. It is the language of heavenly light or the holy third language. Humans can rarely hear it, but it imprints upon them. The plants and animals, even the air and waterways, can hear and sing these songs. They pick up our life songs and resonate with them on Earth and through the skies, onward across all the universes.

"Our songs are our stories. The stone people keep all our stories alive. The crystal children sing them into the Earth's grids and ley lines. That grid now carries unconditional love. Everyone's story will be known and shared in God's true light and love."

These simple words brought tears to Elandra's eyes. She wasn't sure exactly why.

The songbird took to flight and disappeared.

THE ROYAL WEDDING

The coronation day had arrived. The kingdom was crowded with guests of every species. Everyone was welcome and the day shone bright.

Aurora was a vision in layers of white taffeta, satin, and hand-sewn pearls. Jewels glinted at her throat, fingers, and ears. She had mastered the tiny glass slippers. After a lifetime in comfortable riding boots, walking in high heels was no small feat.

Skye was there. She cascaded faery sparkles across Aurora's cheeks and long red tresses. Her eyes sparkled just as brightly as the faery dust. Apanane birds, a distant, later extinct cousin of the hummingbird, darted colorfully about. Unicorns, griffins, dragons, and even the merpeople milled around in fields, crowded streets, and waterways.

Delicate white flowers sweeter than orchids and bigger than lilies composed Aurora's bouquet. Butterflies flicked colorful wings within each bloom. Skye's bouquet was similar, but in soft, pastel colors and fragrances like gardenias and lilacs. It was indeed a glorious day.

A regal Queen Boudica was very pleased. She had seen Elandra in the amulet. She knew her to be housed in love and healing in the kingdom of Zeus. The queen was pleased she was not cut off from her beloved Elandra in this lifetime, despite their differences in time and space. Elandra would be present at the wedding through her amulet sight.

Archers loosed the arrows that foretold the entrance of Queen Boudica. After the nuptials were over, and the prince-who-would-then-be-king had removed Aurora's veil so everyone could see the lost princess who was now queen, Boudica would place her crown upon Aurora's head. *Gladly,* Boudica thought wryly.

Corban and Boudica would be free to pursue their love and live their lives happily ever after, without the interference of status or a caste system of any kind. She giggled, feeling like a young girl in love again.

Queen Boudica took her front-row seat and smiled over at Prince Mahaveritas. He looked handsome, golden, and completely in charge. He would be an excellent king for his people.

Music started, and Boudica noted the "ooohs" and "ahhhs" from those assembled.

Skye flitted down to the altar, inches above the royal red carpet. She was so excited to be the maid of honor that her feet could not touch the ground.

Chasca, as priestess and guardian of divine young love, would dispense the vows, lead the ceremony, and pronounce the good marriage news to all the worlds. Today, this kingdom was restored with its rightful queen and king. The kingdom would go forward, thriving in love. Kindness, peace, and compassion would replace cruelty, war, and fear. The island Kingdom of Mythoses would rise and live again, in its fabled grandeur, if not better.

Princess Devi was smiling out across the crowds. Queen Boudica turned.

Aurora, goddess of the dawn, stood there, looking like the shining light of morning dew. Her ethereal visage was at odds with the inquisitive leaping cat energy she had always displayed. It was a wondrous effect for Aurora had obviously been born into this moment.

Queen Boudica was sobbing. Celestia, sitting next to

her, gave her a nudge and a lacy handkerchief. She had one for herself as well. She smiled through happy tears.

Aurora sedately took her place upon the dais. Bride and groom turned to face their people.

One by one, the seven gifts of the Holy Spirit of the original Mythoses royal bloodline were brought forward and presented to Aurora.

The first was from the Earth Mother, the Seelie queen who announced, "I gift to you the holy scepter."

She lifted a golden, bejeweled scepter. Red rubies and other colorful gems glistened among diamond sparkles. Aurora opened her hands wide, and the Seelie queen of golden light placed it holographically into her root, or first chakra, so it and the other gifts would always descend along the royal bloodline.

"This scepter I have placed within your root and earth chakras to ground you. It brings the gift of wisdom, wealth, and the red heat of passionate living." The queen of the Fae bowed her head and retreated.

The kumari herself presented the next gift. "Into your womb, the chakra of fertility and life, I plant this orange seed. It is the seed of piety. It shall grow in you with godliness, holiness, and reverence for all life, and guarantee you many healthy children."

It, too, was placed holographically within Aurora.

Queen Eithne was the next to step forward. "Darling one, I am honored to present the sword of fortitude. It is golden yellow. I place it within your solar plexus, your center of empowerment, and third chakra. It is for benevolence in the face of war." She, too, bowed and stepped away.

The priestess Chasca came forward. "Dear daughter of

my own lineage, I gift you this shining green emerald, for love, into your heart. I also gift this deeply pink ruby into your high heart. They blend your human love with your higher self 's holy love." With that, two enormous gems of exquisite clarity disappeared holographically into Aurora's fourth chakra.

Queen Clementia took Chasca's place before the couple. "I gift you, daughter, the trumpet of understanding. I place it in your throat, for it is the voice of forgiveness. From your fifth chakra, and out of the clear blue, may you always speak your profound and holy truths."

Aurora had tears sliding down her cheeks, which only served to make her all the more beautiful. Mahaveritas squeezed her hand.

Skye gave her a saucy wink. As intended, it had Rory smiling again.

In all her glory, Queen Elbereth stepped up and smiled. "I give to you this sacred lamp to light your way. Its gift is sight and knowledge." She lovingly placed the small lamp of abalone shell filled with scented oils of deep blue into Aurora's sixth chakra, her third eye, for seeing the unseen. Elbereth kissed the bride on both cheeks. Aurora was truly glowing.

Suddenly there was a confusion of light and sound. They could feel the presence of the great Aum and hear music. A great, glowing orb of golden light appeared before the royal couple. Aurora and Mahaveritas looked directly into the light, although that was hard to do. Many shielded their eyes. The energy had a soft, benign feel. A voice emanated in all their heads.

"We come in bliss. We are the Council of the Holy Light. Some future day, humanity will know us as the

Council of the Christed, but that is a future foretelling. Today, we present you with the council crown, so you may give good counsel in love, patience, kindness, and benevolence for all beings under your rule and those who will follow, from the house of God."

A dazzling sparkle of light seemed to illuminate around Aurora. There were swirls of white and lavender and gold. The orb faded, but the bright aura around the new queen did not. The people cheered.

The beautiful golden Chasca spoke the vows of love, faith, belief, truth, and integrity. She asked the people if they would accept this loving couple as their true and unchallenged queen and king. There was a resounding "yes." People were hugging, crying, and kissing.

Aurora and Mahaveritas took their places as their authentic selves and true flames. As wife and husband. The queen and king. Best and faithful friends forever.

Her new husband turned back her veil and they gazed into each other's smiling eyes. The royal couple kissed, before turning to face their people

Chasca's voice rang clear. "I present to you your queen and king!"

Boudica stood and approached the jubilant pair. She carefully placed her crown upon Aurora's head. Corban handed her a simpler version, which she then placed upon Mahaveritas's head, and stepped back. Everyone smiled at one another.

The royal couple kissed again.

As the kiss ended, a deep bell began to toll. A female voice called out from the back of the crowd. Perplexed, Queen Aurora beckoned the limpid woman forward. She was in shades of sea foam, turquoise, and topaz blue.

Reflecting all the colors of the ocean, she glided like water to the dais.

There she introduced herself as Queen Venelia, the wife of the sea god Neptune.

"Dear people, I have a pronouncement." Even Princess Devi looked surprised.

"My husband, the High Lord of Neptune, departed from his home planet, the place of creativity, magic and spirituality, to come here and help mankind create a beautiful world of their own. King Neptune helped create Mythoses as a paradise. When it's people failed him, he brought destruction upon that original kingdom. What was not destroyed, escaped here, to begin anew. Long have we watched over you, our people of Mythoses past. Much have you learned. We are pleased. You have restored the rightful queen to the throne. It has been done with faith, integrity, and mercy. Even sacrifice.

"I have convinced my husband to show equal mercy. Our wedding gift to this royal couple is that the full isle Kingdom of Mythoses shall rise again from where it slumbers on the ocean floor. In three days' time, after a proper wedding celebration, the seas shall part. Mythoses will arise and you shall rebuild a bigger, better, kinder kingdom upon that land.

"However, no longer will it be known as Mythoses. Going forward, it shall be known as the land of Lemuria, the land of love. It shall survive and know great peace, wisdom, and gentleness. Long will the lineage of Queen Aurora and King Mahaveritas reign. Lemuria will never be shrouded in the black mythology of the banished Mythoses. It shall live anew in equanimity and stand as a crystalline prototype for all the worlds to come."

With that, Queen Venelia kneeled before the newly crowned couple. Everyone dropped to their knees. A roar, like the sound of waves crashing and thunder rolling, came from the calm seas and blue sky. Venelia gaily laughed. She rose to her feet.

"Leave it to my darling Neptune to always get in the last word."

Before the laughter could fade, a colorful rainbow filled the sky. It seemed to end amid the royal festivities. This was a good omen.

From the myriad of colorful light, a figure emerged. Mahaveritas's eyes grew large. He barked out a surprised but delighted laugh. He rushed over to the radiant woman. He clasped this newcomer in his arms and twirled her in several circles as she laughed.

"Mother! By the gods, it has been eons." The thrilled king pulled the woman forward to meet a waiting Aurora.

"My beloved, I present my sacred mother, Veritas, goddess of truth, daughter of planet Saturn and mother of all virtues." The king bowed. The queen curtsied, and the groom's mother bowed her head.

"Daughter of my heart, you have been so long awaited. My son was exiled to his studies so he could become worthy of you and your people. I believe he has done that, and I would not lie."

The people laughed wholeheartedly at both this news and the pun. No, the goddess of truth would not deceive them. This was accepted as a great and worthy sign of completeness.

"It is far that I have come, not only to see my precious son finally wed, but to crown the Princess Devi as Queen of Love on Earth."

The kumari stepped shyly forward. The good mother Veritas took her hands and looked deeply into her huge child eyes.

"Precious daughter, throughout time you have waited. You have waited for the garnishing of enough holy light so that Earth could become your ways of peace and love. I honor you. Heaven and all the heavens do. We thank you for the role you have played in making this royal quest successful. Without that success, Earth would have remained in darkness, perhaps forever."

Veritas indicated with a nod of her head and Queen Celestia moved to stand next to her. She had never glowed so brightly. She had never been more proud of humans than now.

Queen Celestia raised her hands, in which she held a sparkling crystal crown, delicate and reflecting all the colors of the rainbows. The kumari pulled her hands from Veritas's warm clasp, and brought her hands to her mouth. Large tears coursed down her cheeks and love poured from her open heart.

"It is with great honor that I, Queen Celestia, queen of the angels, now crown you Queen of Love, guardian of peace and good will on planet Earth."

The precious crown was placed upon the head of the child, who was now the queen of a new earth. All the people from all the realms roared their delight.

It was time to party!

FESTIVITIES

Amid all the revelry, Aurora found her attention drawn to the single small bird perched upon a castle wall that was gaily festooned with flowers and ribbons. The little thing could barely be seen among all the blooms, but its sweet music drew her. Skye leaned over.

"Do you hear that birdsong?" Skye asked in a reverent voice.

"I do. But what is it? Somehow it seems familiar."

As the two friends listened, another small bird flew in. Then another. Soon, darting birds were the buzz of conversation. The learned king stood and stared in awe at the twittering flock of blue songbirds.

"Those are melanotis. Unusual and rarely seen." He was getting very excited. "These birds can mimic the sounds of other birds, animals, and even the whistling and singing of people. This is a great omen, indeed."

The first blue songbird left its perch and hopped onto the table, directly in front of Queen Aurora and Skye, and began to sing. The other birds joined in chorus. Skye felt a thrill run up her spine and turned to Aurora. The queen's eyes widened and she turned to stare at Skye.

"Is it true? Am I hearing Elandra's name in that song?"

Skye nodded, too overcome to speak. She cocked her head to listen closely. "I can hear all our names in the songbird's story."

The king sat back down in his chair, dazed.

Queen Devi smiled and lifted her hand. The joyous songbird alighted on her finger. The two seemed deep in conversation. The queen of love laughed.

"This pretty blue songbird has arrived from Mount Olympus. That is where our Elandra is now residing. That kingdom of gods and goddesses has begun to tell our tale, far and wide.

"This little bird has learned the story of our great quest. She knows the roles we each have played. She knows how the warrior Elandra fell and Heaven wept. She sings about the fall and now the rise and restoration of the new Mythoses kingdom, known to all as Lemuria. Her story holds all the love and devotion this royal couple brings to the kingdom and each other. Our songs are being sung, and the universe is responding." Queen Devi was thrilled.

"Forevermore, the song of Elandra will be sung upon the winds, resonating within the trees and the grasses. This tale will be told in all the elements—air, water, fire, earth, wood, and metal. The ethers shall be your scribes. What has been done will forever be known and celebrated. Elandra is as alive upon the wind as one could ever be here, with feet planted upon the ground.

"Do you understand this moment? As this great tale is sung, you—we—are all forever. We are eternally alive, as our songs can never cease. They only grow longer. These precious birds have preserved the legends from Olympus and set them loose upon our Earth. Elandra is once again and for all times."

The queens of the roundtable, queens from all the realms, arose and began to clap.

...And they all lived happily ever after...

EPILOGUE

Elandra, staring deeply into her precious amulet, heard every word. The little bird who had flown to Earth had blessed her with eternity. She felt content.

Elandra decided she could look forward to more lifetimes. Not just a life of being Joan whatever-her-name-was but many lifetimes. She would seek and find her twin flame, Elthaneos every time. They would create in a world of love, goodness, and truehearted righteousness.

Life truly was a complicated game of hide-and-seek, and she was ready to play! *After all, who am I to argue with God?* Elandra mused.

For one quick moment, Elandra was almost sure she heard God laughing out loud.

The End
...Until the next beginning...

Watch for the newest adventures of Elandra and her
ethereal companions, coming soon in:
The Art of Betrayal: Another Timeless Fairytale
Book Two of the Spiritual Warrior Trilogy

ART OF BEAUTY BOOK STUDY AND DISCUSSION QUESTIONS:

Why or why not?

1. Do you believe faeries and other elemental groups of beings actually exist today? Have you had personal experiences with any?

2. Was King Neptune justified in sinking the Isle of Mythoses and punishing her people?

3. Do you believe in prophecy, fate, or free will choice?

4. Do witches still exist today? Is Wicca a pagan religion of light or a slippery slope to darker arts? Discuss.

5. Do the Seven Heavenly Virtues exist as energies, beings, indoctrination or emotions?

6. Was Skye justified in killing the troll-ogre after he killed Aethelwyn?

7. Do you believe Atlantis existed? Lemuria?

8. Do you believe humans can shape-shift like Aurora could change into a lioness and Marisha was changed into a phoenix?

9. When people hide their true selves and motives behind charisma, kindness or "gaslighting", is this a modern day type of "shape-shifting"?

10. Do you believe we are descended from Star Beings? That we are "star seeds"? Do you believe in extraterrestrials?

11. Do you believe we all leave a resonance or "song" upon the earth that exemplifies our life?

12. Should Elandra have been admitted back to Heaven? What do you believe happens when we die?

13. Is Mount Olympus, as a "half-way heaven" a real place? Is it a purgatory?

14. Who was your favorite character of the three warrior women and why?

ABOUT THE AUTHOR

Ellen lives with her beloved husband, Thane, in what they call their "slice of Eden." A licensed disc jockey, she later trained as a journalist, then lawyer. She and her recently retired dentist husband have moved to the delightful Gulf Coast community of Venice, Florida, drawn by sunny weather, beaches, and sunsets.

Proud parents and grandparents, Thane and Ellen live an earth-friendly, shamanic lifestyle in their open and supportive community. Visit them at www.stonewisdom.net, where you will also find Ellen's blog. Ellen claims eclectic research, and many spiritual inputs contributed to this book (and trilogy), which she refers to as Spiritual Fiction. Another magical fairytale romance, The Art of Betrayal, is already in the works.

Ellen can be reached at stonewisdom555@yahoo.com. Don't miss Ellen's Divine Whisperings, child-friendly, sleep relaxation programs for the entire family coming to YouTube.

Learn more at www.stonewisdom.net.

The Spiritual Warrior Trilogy and Divine Whisperings
Copyright©2019 Ellen Ostroth

Made in the USA
Lexington, KY
13 August 2019